Roger The Mini-Dragon And The Magic Meadow

Roger The Mini-Dragon And The Magic Meadow

Trish Sardinha

iUniverse®

ROGER THE MINI-DRAGON AND THE MAGIC MEADOW

iUniverse books may be ordered through booksellers or by contacting:

iUniverse
1663 Liberty Drive
Bloomington, IN 47403
www.iuniverse.com
1-800-Authors (1-800-288-4677)

ISBN: 978-1-4917-9373-2 (sc)
ISBN: 978-1-4917-9375-6 (hc)
ISBN: 978-1-4917-9374-9 (e)

Print information available on the last page.

iUniverse rev. date: 07/27/2016

Chapter 1

Introducing Roger the Dragon

It was spring in Calgary, Alberta, but the temperatures could range from below zero Celsius to plus thirty. Fortunately, the weather gods were smiling on this oil town on this particular day, and the weather was balmy. This was especially fortunate for new lives commencing—birds, bugs, various critters, and dragons.

"Dragons?" you ask, a wee bit puzzled, perhaps even shaking your head a bit. Nevertheless, yes, you heard correctly; dragons did exist in certain sleepy, hidden hollows in the heart of the thriving city. One in particular comes to mind; his name was Roger.

There is a natural park sheltered within the community of Varsity, in Calgary. It is, without a doubt, breathtaking. The landscape is vast; there are woods and hills, flowers, and wildlife everywhere. One of the city's rivers winds its frothy, riotous way through the valley of this Atlantis. This paradise thrives within the city, but it has its secrets, its unknown depths and unraveled layers. Hence, we encounter certain species that are not usually common in the modern world. Enter, stage left, Roger.

Roger's mother was a miniature dragon. She existed centuries ago. She lived quite comfortably with the dinosaurs. She resembled these massive creatures in appearance (if not in size) but was never documented as one of their species. Her bones were not preserved. She simply faded away. Before her time in this reality ended, however, she laid her eggs. Most of her offspring perished with the dinosaurs; however, one egg got lost. With the planet evolving, the earth shifting, this little egg tumbled, rolled, and eventually settled in a tiny nook.

The egg was buried and preserved. Yes, centuries passed, the earth shifted again and again, but this little egg survived. It resurfaced into a strange new world; dinosaurs were long extinct. Humans, arguably the most deadly species on the planet, were in the process of causing most of the remaining life-forms to become extinct—including themselves. It was not, perhaps, the most ideal place for a small, bedraggled mythical creature.

Ideal or not, Roger hatched. On this sunny spring day, the egg, which had sheltered Roger for so many centuries, was hiccupped to the surface. The enamel started to crack. This tiny prehistoric critter scratched and clawed his way into that strange new world. Once he could move, Roger scrambled out of the brambles and crawled to the top of the ridge.

Roger (well, he thought of that name later) was exhausted from his struggle to remove himself from his leathery prison and his clamber up the cliff. It had not been a long climb, but he was newly hatched after all. Essentially, his young being had been sleeping until the environmental conditions spurred him to life. He was curled in a tight spring on the spongy ground. His eyes were squeezed shut. His fragile wings plastered to his tiny frame, he was completely bewildered, lonely, and … hungry.

This lovely natural park was host to many, many critters, but it had never encountered a wrinkly, winged, clawed, and toothsome beastie like our hero, Roger. Roger had yet to open his eyes and hence was unaware that several of these critters had assembled around him, until one of them spoke. When Roger heard this voice, his bright eyes flew open in surprise. He peered at the group around him. It must be said that after having been buried in the earth for so long, Roger had absorbed much of its knowledge and history. Roger hence knew what these critters were. Roger remained silent and listened curiously.

It was an old hare who had spoken initially.

"My esteemed colleagues," the hare began, "it appears that we have an intruder in our midst."

"I doubt he meant to intrude, if you catch my drift," volunteered a crow.

"He looks scared," mentioned a black squirrel.

The hare cleared his throat. "Perhaps we should try to determine what it is and who it belongs to. We can't just leave it here, defenseless—something may get at it."

Roger noticed that the hare gave a coyote a pointed look.

"I'm not about to sink my teeth into that!" snapped the coyote. "Thanks a lot! I do have some savvy … never tried to eat you, did I?"

"He's too fast and stringy for you," laughed the squirrel. "You prefer the neighborhood dogs: soft, fat, and *slow*."

The coyote made a show of delicately licking his paws and settled back on his haunches. "I will not dignify that with a response," he told the squirrel.

Roger had been watching and listening to the interactions with some interest. Now, by some perverse law of nature, all but the human animal can communicate with each other instantly. Roger had understood every word this crowd in front of him had said. He scrambled to his feet.

"Who are you?" Roger blurted. "And who am I?"

"Oh, hello," said the crow. "We didn't realize you were awake. We're not even sure *what* you are, much less who you are. You don't have a name?"

A name suddenly popped into Roger's head. Possibly his mother had named her eggs, those many centuries ago, and it had sunk into his sleeping mind, along with his knowledge of the earth.

"I am Roger," he declared.

"Roger is a fine name," the crow replied. "I am Soot, and that is Tip." Soot pointed to the old hare. "This is Patch." The squirrel waved his tail. "And Jasper." The coyote bowed his head politely.

"Where did you come from, Roger?" asked Soot curiously. "We just saw you lying on the ridge."

"I remember clawing out of something and then climbing up here."

"What did you claw out of?" This time it was Tip asking the question.

"I'll show you," Roger replied. Roger led the group to edge of the cliffs. He pointed to the leathery, blackish-green egg nestled on a shelf below.

"That looks like an egg," Soot ventured, "although it's not like anything I've ever seen before."

"I've never seen anyone looking like you, Roger, on the ridge or anywhere else," Tip added. "Do you have a mum?"

"I don't know," Roger stammered in reply.

"I suspect she is no longer around," Jasper said, "or she'd have been looking for you."

"We'll look after you," Tip assured Roger, "at least until your mum shows up."

"I don't think she will," Roger said glumly. "I think I was in that egg for a very long time. It's just a feeling I have."

"You may be right, Roger," Tip said. "As I mentioned, I've never seen anyone like you before."

"Nor have we," the others all chimed, in chorus. "So you just remain with us, Roger."

Roger looked at the assorted critters around him and decided it would be quite all right to stay with them. He did, however, have a couple of questions concerning the initial conversation he heard.

"What did you mean about me being defenseless and that something might get at me?" Roger asked Tip. "And why did you look at Jasper?"

"Without a mum or us to look after you, there are certain other animals who might try to eat you," Tip replied uncomfortably. "I was just teasing Jasper when I looked at him. Jasper is not like most coyotes."

Jasper interrupted. "Many of my kind are not very nice and eat smaller animals, such as those little dogs Patch referred to," he began. "I guess I am unusual; I prefer nuts and berries, and certain leafy greens from the forest, plus the occasional fish."

"I can be a bit hasty with my comments," Tip said. "I've been around for so long I am almost a fixture in the woods. I sometimes fool myself into thinking I can get away with saying anything."

"Yes," agreed Patch. "You *can* be a pompous rabbit at times, and I can be a terrible tease; we squirrels like to chatter."

"We're all good friends, Roger," Soot said. "We do occasionally tease one another, but it's friendly teasing."

Roger sensed that he was indeed amongst a group of good friends. He did not feel alone or scared anymore. Roger did wonder about his mum; he had a feeling that he would never meet her, so it was good to be among friends. This was a new world for him; he was glad these critters had found him. He told them so and watched in amusement as they all seemed to fluff themselves up with pride.

Roger sensed something else; he had an odd sensation in his tummy, which he recognized as hunger. The same hunger he had felt after climbing to the ridge, but his little dragon tummy was rumbling with greater force than before. He was just about to ask about finding something to eat when he heard Soot give a startled cry.

"I see Sheila!" Soot exclaimed.

"Sheila is not supposed to be out!" Jasper cried.

Roger watched as a large brown dog galloped up. She did not look like Jasper. Roger looked for Jasper, to reaffirm his comparison. Much to his surprise and dismay, the coyote was gone. Upon further scrutiny, he noticed that *all* of his new friends were no longer to be seen. Roger stared up at the new creature with his bright green-gold eyes. His little dragon heart was fluttering heavily in his chest, and his hunger was forgotten in his fear.

Chapter 2

Roger Meets Sheila and Her Boys

R oger, heart still pounding, was wondering if this large dog was a
critter that might like to have him for a snack.

"Please don't eat me!" he said in a small voice.

The dog pulled back her head and gave Roger a surprised look.

"Eat you!" she exclaimed. "I'm not going to eat you; you don't look
very edible anyway. You're sort of scaly."

"Oh, I'm not edible at all," Roger hastily replied.

"My name is Sheila," said the dog. "Who are you?"

"I'm Roger. I came out of an egg on the ridge and climbed up here."

"You hatched from an egg? I've never seen a bird that looks like you."

"I don't think I'm a bird," Roger said. "I'm just not certain *what* I am. I don't look like anyone I've met so far."

"Who *have* you met so far?" asked Sheila, looking around. "I don't see anyone else out here."

Roger told her about meeting Tip and the others.

"They were all so nice," Roger said miserably. "They said they would look after me, since I have no mother. Now they've left."

"You don't have a mother?" Sheila asked sadly.

"No. I think I was in the egg a long time, and she is gone." Roger repeated what he had told his friends.

"I do not know your friends well, but I cannot imagine that they would abandon you," Sheila said. "I bet they got spooked when they saw me. I am not usually out of my yard on my own." Sheila looked around again, and Roger saw her start.

"Oh no," she moaned. "Here come my boys. They'll want to take me home."

Roger followed Sheila's gaze and watched in surprise as two young humans raced in their direction. The boys stopped in front of Roger and Sheila. Both boys stared at Roger; their mouths were wide open.

"What do you suppose that is?" one of the boys said.

"I don't know. It's weird looking whatever it is," the other lad replied.

Roger gazed up at the two boys and with as much dignity as he could muster stammered: "I am not an *it*. I am Roger."

The boys looked at Roger in surprise.

"Did you just speak?" one of them asked. He looked at his friend and said, "I must have been playing on the computer too late last night."

"I heard him, too," the other boy replied, "We *must* have been playing too long."

****

The boys were still young enough to believe in magic, which was why they could understand our friend Roger. Roger was nothing if not magical. It was also due to their youth that they recovered quite quickly from their initial shock and became very curious.

****

Roger waited patiently for the boys to finish before calmly saying, "I can hear you as well, and I know *I* wasn't playing on a computer, whatever that is, last night. I just hatched, over there." Roger waved his scaly little arm at the ridge.

"I'm Mark," one of the boys said.

"And I'm Matthew," the other said. "You said that you hatched?"

"Are you some kind of lizard?" Mark asked Roger.

"You look more like a dragon," Matthew said thoughtfully.

"You definitely must get more sleep," Mark told Matthew, "a dragon indeed."

Roger, however, had a sudden insight. *Maybe I am a dragon*, he thought. *That would certainly explain why I don't look like anyone else.*

"I *was* hatched," Roger replied, once he was finally allowed to speak again. He was just about to repeat the story of his discovery when Sheila barked a warning. Roger saw other young humans entering the park. He looked up at Mark and Matthew questioningly.

"One of us should take you home, Roger. We should go before anyone else sees you," Mark said.

"I can take him," Matthew volunteered.

Roger saw Sheila give Matthew a sharp look. Before he knew what was happening, Sheila had picked him up by the scruff of his neck and tossed him onto her back.

"Hang on, Roger," Sheila barked. She started running toward the edge of the park—the boys in hot pursuit.

"Where are we going?" Roger asked Sheila, baffled. "Why did we have to leave the ridge?"

"We're going to my house," Sheila replied. "We had to leave the ridge to keep you safe. I didn't want the other humans to find you, and I didn't want Matthew to take you."

"What if my friends come looking for me?" Roger asked next.

"I don't think they would go to that area when humans are there."

"Why couldn't I go with Matthew?"

"It's not exactly safe at Matthew's house," Sheila said quietly. "But you shall be fine here. We're home." Sheila had stopped at a large gate. She sat Roger down gently and pushed the gate open with her nose.

"This is how I got out," she explained. Sheila gently picked up Roger again and trotted over to a strange, enclosed structure that was full of plants. In his admittedly very brief existence thus far, Roger had only seen greenery that grew outside.

"What is that?" Roger asked Sheila.

"That is a greenhouse, "Sheila replied. "A greenhouse is full of leafy, growing things. You'll be fine in here." Sheila nudged open the greenhouse door with her nose, (now, come on, you know our four-legged friends have more tricks up their little snouts than they let on) and plunked a bewildered Roger in one of the plants.

"Please try to stay hidden," Sheila said. "There is someone else who stays here; she looks after Mark and me. Her name is Gail. I am not certain what her reaction would be if she saw you, if she could even see you. Many humans do not see the magic around them—including the fact that all living creatures talk—even the plants and the trees. They rarely stop to listen to, much less understand, the conversations going on all around them. I find it curious that Mark and Matthew seem to understand you, Roger; they certainly do not understand me. Maybe it is because you are very magical—almost like you are from a different world.

"Whoops, I hear the boys coming now; I had better leave. I'll come back as soon as I can."

Roger watched as Sheila backed out of the greenhouse and pulled the door closed with her teeth. Roger was quite content to be alone with the leafy beings. He could almost hear them rustling, whispering and sighing to each other; in fact, when his hunger returned, and he attempted to nibble on a leaf, he thought he heard the plant talk.

"Stop that!" it said irritably. "I am a hibiscus and quite rare to these parts, I'll have you know."

Roger quickly stopped his nibbling and glanced around the greenhouse. "What shall I do with myself?" He stood up carefully, so as not to disturb the hibiscus. His legs were no longer wobbly, and his wings—his wings—he could extend them like the branches on the hibiscus. Roger, to his amazement and joy, could actually use those webby burdens attached to his side to fly.

Now, like any young fledgling, Roger had no idea how to fly, and he had no nurturing feathered mum to show him. Roger, however, was not afraid. He wiggled his wings (proudly, because he could), strained on his lizard legs, and propelled himself off the hibiscus, right on to the floor of the greenhouse—ouch. Roger dragged himself up. He was a wee bit embarrassed but still proud. He was startled to see Sheila staring down at him.

"When did you get back?" Roger stammered.

"I came in just now. Are you hurt?" Sheila asked Roger. "How did you get down there? Did you fall?"

"No, I'm not hurt. I was using these," Roger replied. Roger waved his wings.

"You were trying to use your wings to fly," Sheila said. "I was *wondering* if you could fly."

"Yes!" Roger agreed triumphantly. "I was trying to fly, although not very well as it turns out."

"That's great, Roger!" said Sheila. "I don't think you should be flying a lot in here, though. There is not much space, and I did caution you to remain out of sight. Do you think you can try to stay in one place for now? I've brought you something to eat."

"I'll stay put," Roger told her, "and thank you. I *am* hungry. I'll just fly back up to that plant." Roger was preparing to launch himself back, *gently*, into the hibiscus, when Sheila began swiveling her head from side to side, as if trying to make a decision.

"Would you mind moving to that plant over there?" Sheila pointed her snout toward a gigantic plant with huge leaves. "It will provide better cover for you."

Roger flapped his wings and flew into the larger plant. It did have much bigger leaves, he noted, than the hibiscus. He settled his scaly little self far behind a huge leaf.

Roger watched happily as Sheila shook the contents of a bag (potato chips) in front of him.

"That's all I could manage for now," she said apologetically. "But I'll bring you something else to eat later."

"Sheila?" Roger ventured, stopping her before she left again. "Thank you for bringing me here and for getting me something to eat. I am still worried that if my friends come looking for me, they will not be able to find me. *If* they come looking for me, that is. I know they ran away on the ridge, but you said that you had probably scared them?"

"I'm sure they will look for you," Sheila replied. "Soot and Patch *do* come by the yard. When I next see them, I will tell them where you are." After a pause, Sheila said, "There is another bird, as well, who is also around the yard on many occasions. His name is Jack; he is a blue jay. I think I may have heard his cry outside as I was entering the greenhouse. For now, eat your snack and try to rest."

Roger was very much relieved by Sheila's answer. He burrowed himself further beneath the broad leaves of the plant and started on his snack. He found the chips very much to his liking. It had been a busy day for a newborn dragon, and after consuming all of the chips, Roger felt sleepy. He instinctively curled his diminutive wings around himself and fell asleep.

Chapter 3

Jack the Jay
Discovers Roger

J ack the blue jay was flying over Sheila's yard, occasionally uttering his raucous, slightly mournful cry, when he spotted Sheila far below. She appeared to be going into the greenhouse.

Now, that is interesting, Jack thought. He swooped down to take a better look, landed on a branch close to the greenhouse, and gazed in. Much to his surprise, she appeared to be speaking to a leaf, and the leaf had eyes—large green-gold eyes! Jack had come upon Sheila just as she was giving Roger his snack.

This really is interesting. I must share this with my friends, Jack thought. He flew off to the ridge and spotted his friends immediately. They seemed to be milling about rather aimlessly, and as he approached, he heard bits of their conversation.

"I should have stayed with him," Tip grumbled.

"Well, old boy," said Soot. "You are getting on in years. If Sheila got it into her head to give you a chase, well …"

"Sheila wouldn't hurt a fly," Patch piped up. "Why, there's many a time I've raided the bird feeders in Sheila's yard, and she's not barked once."

"Yet we took off anyway," Soot said. "We left poor Roger all alone."

"I wonder where he is," said Jasper.

"We should try to find him!" Tip exclaimed.

What a very curious discussion, thought Jack. He gave a cry to announce his arrival before landing on the ridge in front of his friends.

"Hi," chirped Jack. "What's going on? I heard some very interesting conversation as I was flying down. You know how I like to be kept informed about what's going on." Everyone suddenly avoided looking at him.

Tip finally cleared his throat and reported, "Well, we were just gadding about here on the ridge, as we do, and suddenly there was this little lizard-like thing. His name is Roger. He was very young, no obvious mum about, so we said we'd look after him …" Tips voice trailed off.

"And?" prompted Jack.

"And Sheila showed up followed by her boys," Soot added miserably.

"And what happened next?" Jack asked.

"And we all kind of ran away," Jasper finished, not looking at Jack. "We should have stayed," he added.

"You ran away," Jack repeated, in a flat tone. "Did you happen to take Roger with you?"

"No, we left him," Soot responded, ashamed.

Jack was beginning to understand why the leaf that Sheila was talking to had eyes. He knew very well where Roger had ended up, but he wanted to make his comrades squirm a bit.

"You left him!" Jack exclaimed. "You left a helpless, motherless babe."

"Well," whined Patch, who had yet to speak, "we thought maybe his mum would show up, and he'd be fine." Jack suspected that this last comment was a complete and utter falsehood.

"Uh huh," Jack continued. "Doubtful," he sang. "So, what's your next step? Do you think he still alive, or did you leave him so something would eat him and relieve you of responsibility?"

"No, no, no!" Tip exclaimed. "We're going to go look for him."

"Any idea where?" asked Jack. "Maybe he tumbled off the cliff."

Jack finally decided to take pity on his friends. They were all very upset. They were obviously concerned about Roger and sincere about finding him.

"You haven't asked me what *I* am doing here," Jack said.

"What *are* you doing here, Jack?" It was a collective question from the entire group. They were relieved at what they thought would be a change of subject.

"Well," he replied, "I happened to be flying over Sheila's yard, and I saw her breaking into her people's greenhouse. *Now, why would she do that?* I asked myself. I flew a little closer and saw her talking to a leaf."

"A leaf?" they all responded.

"With eyes," Jack replied.

"A leaf with eyes?" repeated Jasper. "Did you eat a bad nut?"

"Now why do you think that leaf had eyes?" Jack prompted, ignoring Jasper's comment.

"Oh! You think Roger is in the greenhouse with Sheila," Tip said.

"I do," said Jack. "I think he'll be perfectly safe there, too. Sheila will look after him. But you all should be ashamed of yourselves!"

"We should go make sure he's all right," Tip suggested.

"That's a good plan," Jack replied. "We birds and Patch will go. We'll fly and scramble over there, check on Roger, and report back."

"Come on, you lot," he encouraged, and off he flew. Soot took off after him. Patch scurried along too.

Jack and Soot were perched on branches in Sheila's yard, waiting for Patch to arrive—Jack always forgot that Patch did not have wings. Sheila's yard was not far from the ridge, so the others had arrived rather quickly. Patch finally clambered onto a branch somewhat lower than the birds.

"What do we do now?" Patch gasped (he was a little out of breath).

"You run to the branch overlooking the greenhouse and try to look in," Jack replied. "We'll have to think of something that will get Sheila out."

"Okay," Patch agreed. With that, he scurried his furry self down the tree he was in and scrambled up another tree with a branch very near the greenhouse.

"Here's what we do," Jack said to Soot. "We cannot make it look too odd—we normally don't fly around together in Sheila's yard. Soot, if you land right outside on the deck and caw loudly, it might attract attention. Patch and I will meet you at the greenhouse. Maybe we'll see Roger."

Soot flew to the deck at the back of Sheila's house. He started cawing loudly. Jack watched from the greenhouse, and to his satisfaction, shortly after Soot had commenced his performance, Sheila flew out of the house.

"Hello, Sheila," Soot said.

"Hello, yourself," snapped Sheila. "What are you doing here?"

"We came to find Roger," said Jack, having flown back from the greenhouse.

"How do you know that this Roger is here?" asked Sheila.

Jack repeated to Sheila what he had told his friends.

"Roger *is* in the greenhouse," Sheila admitted. "How could you leave him on the ridge?"

Sheila's question was addressed to Soot, and Soot seemed uncomfortable. Jack decided to help Soot out. "You startled them," Jack told Sheila. "They *were* going to look for him when I showed up and told them about the eyes in the leaf."

"That's what I told Roger, that I probably startled his friends," Sheila said, relenting. "Come on. I'll sneak you all into the greenhouse to see Roger."

"Let's go then," Jack said. He was happy that things were working out, not only for his friends but also for Roger. He was very much looking forward to meeting the little dragon.

Chapter 4

Roger Is Reunited with His Friends

Roger woke from his snooze to find Sheila's large brown eyes staring at him once again. To his amazement and delight, he saw Soot, Patch, and an unfamiliar blue jay perched on various branches in the greenhouse.

"You found me!" he exclaimed happily.

"Jack found you," said Sheila, and she introduced Jack to Roger.

"It was accidental," Jack said. He told Roger the entire story.

"You *were* going to look for me!" cried Roger. He looked happily at his friends. Having spent some time with Sheila and discovering how friendly she was, Roger wondered why his friends had run away from her earlier.

I am new to this world, he reminded himself. *I have a lot to learn.* Roger gave himself a mental shake as he realized that a couple of his friends were missing.

"Where are Tip and Jasper?" he asked. "Did they not want to find me?"

"Of course they did!" replied Jack. "Jasper never goes into any areas where humans live. Tip cannot get into Sheila's yard. I'm sure you'll see them again."

"Sheila told me she had to bring me home so other humans wouldn't find me," Roger ventured. "Mark and Matthew are humans. They seemed nice to me."

"Mark is my boy, and Matthew is his friend," Sheila said. "I know them and trust them, but I do not know too many other humans. I was not going to leave you alone with strangers."

Roger remembered that Sheila had said that Matthew's house was not safe, but he decided not to ask her about it. Roger also wondered what he should do now. Should he stay in the greenhouse or go back with his friends? He did not know if he could keep up with his friends; his webby legs were short, and he had not practiced flying. He was thus relieved when Jack spoke. Jack seemed to have read his mind.

"You seem comfortable, Roger," Jack said. "I am relieved Sheila brought you to the greenhouse. Would you like to stay here for a while? It is not that I don't want you with us; I'm simply not certain *how* you would get back to the ridge. Maybe when you are stronger and have learned how to fly?"

"You mean when I can fly better?" Roger asked. He noted the stunned expressions on the faces around him and realized that his friends were not aware that he *could* fly already (except for Sheila, of course). "I can fly," he said. "I'm just not very good at it yet. I *am* comfortable here, and I *would* probably slow you down right now. I would like to stay here." Roger looked at Sheila and asked, "Is that all right with you, Sheila?"

"I think that would work out nicely. I would feel better with you in here rather than outside on the ridge," replied Sheila. "I was *also* wondering how you would get back there. Even if I got out and took you to the ridge, you would still have to get around."

"When your wings get stronger, you can fly out to the ridge with us and see Tip and Jasper, too!" enthused Jack.

"In the meantime, we'll come and visit you often!" said Patch.

"You don't mind them visiting, do you, Sheila?" Roger asked Sheila pleadingly.

"No, I don't mind them visiting. They're here quite often anyway," Sheila replied. "They like our new birdfeeder," she added slyly.

"The only thing is, Roger, I don't really like being in the greenhouse," Patch confessed. "It's too confining. I'm here now because I wanted to see you." Patch addressed the others. "Do the rest of you agree?" They all said that they too shared Patch's view of the greenhouse.

"We'll be right outside where you can see us and hopefully hear us," Soot said.

"Will I be able to go outside?" Roger asked Sheila. He was grateful for having a safe home and was grateful that his friends would visit. He would just prefer to visit with them outside rather than through the clear walls of the greenhouse. In addition, since there was not a great deal of room in the greenhouse, he would need to be outside to strengthen his wings. Once again, a friend seemed to be reading his mind.

"You need to strengthen your wings," Sheila replied. "You'll have to be outside for that. I'll figure something out."

"Roger," said Jack, "we should actually get out of here now and let Tip and Jasper know that you are okay."

Roger bid his friends farewell and watched them fly and scamper out of the greenhouse. He was a bit sad to see them go but knew he would see them again. He was also feeling a bit sleepy again and quite hungry. He asked Sheila, shyly, if he could get something else to eat.

"I'm sorry, Roger!" Sheila cried. "With your friends arriving, I completely forgot. I will be right back!" Sheila flew out of the greenhouse and, true to her word, returned quickly. She was carrying something that smelled delicious.

"This is pizza," Sheila told Roger. She gave him two pieces that she had carefully carried in her mouth. "I hope you like it."

"Thank you," Roger said. He easily picked up a piece with one of his front paws and sampled it. It was very much to his liking. He liked it even better than the chips. He shared this tidbit with Sheila.

"I'm glad you like it, Roger. I must go inside now. I will be back tomorrow morning. Will you be all right?"

"Yes," replied Roger, already onto his second slice. "Thank you again!"

"Good night then," Sheila called before slipping away back to the house.

Roger finished his second slice, yawned, and settled back down under the broad leaves of the philodendron. He fell into a deep sleep. His dreams were oddly not filled with his new friends, chips, or pizza; Roger dreamt instead of a huge meadow, filled with flowers.

Chapter 5

Roger and the Eagles

Roger slept right through until the next morning, quite hidden by the philodendron. He was eventually roused from his sleepy state by a rather intriguing aroma flirting with the air. *Hmmm*, he thought. While *kind of* keeping Sheila's warnings about staying hidden in the back of his mind, he *kind of* peeked out from the leaf. A new day had begun.

For Roger, who had been buried for eons, it was not really a new day, but it was another day to explore. He was especially interested in exploring this lovely fragrance, because he was quite hungry, and the fragrance smelled edible. Roger sniffed at the greenery surrounding him;

the fragrance was definitely not coming from the leaves. He was just about to ignore Sheila's warning about staying hidden, so he could find out where the aroma *was* coming from, when Sheila appeared.

"Hi, Roger," Sheila said. "I hope you had a good night. I've brought you breakfast; they're fresh muffins." Sheila was holding two large blueberry muffins carefully by their wrappers. She set them by Roger's feet.

Roger's eyes became even larger (if you can believe it); the muffins were the cause of that lovely fragrance. He picked one up and took a big bite; it was quite delicious—wrapper and all.

"I don't think my people eat that papery thing around the muffin," Sheila said.

"Oh." Roger used a claw on his left paw (yes, he was left pawed) to peel away the paper wrapping and took another bite. "Yes, this is better. Thank you, Sheila! I could smell these, and I was so-o-o hungry." He did *not* mention that he had been on the verge of leaving his hiding place to find the source of the smell before she arrived.

"You're welcome, Roger," Sheila replied. "Gail was baking this morning, and she left the muffins out for Mark. It was easy for me to grab a couple. I usually have better manners than that, but I've got to look after you."

"Everyone is away this morning, and I'll probably have to go inside," Sheila continued as Roger gratefully gobbled his second muffin. "I think it would be safe for you to explore a bit in here. It is not a large space, but you can exercise those wings, a little bit anyway. Just be careful of the plants, please."

Someone outside called Sheila's name.

"That's Gail," she said. "I have to go. I'll see you later."

Sheila's tail vanished through the greenhouse door. Roger took a second look; the door was open. Roger's fear from the previous day had pretty much vanished. He eyed the open door with interest. *If I just fly out quickly*, he thought, *stretch my wings a bit, and fly right back in, that should be okay.* Having thus convinced himself, Roger flexed his webby wings and flew out the door.

*****

Calgary is a beautiful city, with robin-egg-blue skies, snow—sometimes eight months out of the year, not exactly eternal spring, sometimes not a spring at all. The leaves barely blink alive, and winter has descended again.

Calgary is also blessed with a weather system called a chinook. A chinook is a warming wind from the ocean. It has been named snow-eater, because a very strong chinook can melt as much as a foot of snow. The snow-eater usually comes hand in hand with a chinook arch, a band of dark cloud over light, which in Calgary appears in the west, over the mountains.

On the morning that Roger decided to venture out of the open greenhouse, a chinook was galloping down the slopes of those towering rock giants. The chinook was building itself up into a glorious snow-eating feast. It has to be said that there was no snow at the time, but the chinook arrived. Roger flew straight into its warm embrace.

*****

Roger flew carefully out of the greenhouse, only to find himself literally blown away. His wings, although getting stronger by the minute, were no match for the playful wind. The wind tossed him here and there like a basketball. He smacked into a tree in Sheila's yard, and then the wind grabbed him again and hurtled him directly to the ridge.

The wind finally relented and tossed him into some rather woody branches. Roger shook himself off and took a good look around. His little magical, prehistoric self was suddenly overwhelmed, for what he saw was so beautiful: the river, far below, was a turquoise ribbon, trilling like a harp, and the birds sang a boisterous chorus. He also became aware of other sounds that did not sound *quite* so pleasant. He sensed that whatever tree he had landed in was *not* that happy with him being there. Sadly, he soon realized he was correct; the branches beneath Roger suddenly shook violently, and he was tossed abruptly onto the ground, landing on his head.

After recovering, Roger found himself staring into the very scary eyes of a very large bird. He looked nothing like anyone he had met so far. The bird was magnificent. Roger searched his ancient memory bank, and the word *eagle* leapt out at him. Not for the first time, Roger wondered why *dragon* had not popped into his head when asked what *he* was.

"I saw you take your tumble from the tree and flew down to check it out," the eagle said. "What *are* you? You look rather like some kind of hawk."

He peered at Roger closely.

Roger, rather wobbly from being dropped on his head, still knew he had to be quite polite to this grand being. He looked up into his fierce eyes and at his daunting beak. "You're an eagle, and I'm a dragon—I think. My name is Roger."

The eagle, because he *was* in fact an eagle, blinked at Roger.

"Welcome, Roger the dragon," the huge bird said. "My name is Mel. Where did you come from? How did you end up here?"

"I came from up there." Roger pointed to the ridge and then told the eagle about being found and about flying out of the greenhouse. "I was just going to practice flying a bit, and I got blown away," Roger said.

"You were caught up in a chinook," Mel said. "I think you did very well for a youngster. Would you like to fly up with me and see our nest? I am very proud of the nest. We bald eagles build the largest and highest nests of any other bird around here. We can see for miles and more. The wind has died down, so you should be fine. Just follow me."

Mel spread his wings and flew up, and up, and up. "Come on," he encouraged Roger as he swept along after him.

Upward they soared. Roger had found his feet, or his wings in this case, and easily kept pace with the eagle. The nest was huge and held three other eagles. The eagles looked up in surprise as Roger landed in the nest.

"Everyone, this is Roger the dragon," Mel told the others. "Roger, this is my wife, Mildred, and the little ones are Max and Billy."

"Hello, Roger," said Mildred. Roger thought that Mildred and Mel made a good couple; they were *both* magnificent (and imposing).

"Ma, we're hungry," the little ones whined, while gazing curiously at Roger.

"Please excuse them," said Mel. "They are too young to leave the nest yet. Either Mildred or I fish for their meals, while the other looks after them. I was just going for lunch, when I spotted your tumble. I should get back to it, as the lads are hungry. You are probably hungry as well, Roger, after all that bashing about in the chinook. Would you like to go fishing with me?"

"I don't know how to fish, but I *am* hungry; sure, thanks!"

Out of the nest they flew, down to the glistening river below.

"Now," Mel cautioned, as they swirled down, "the trick is to grab a fish out of the water, with your claws. You must be careful not to grab too large a fish, or it can drag you under." Mel demonstrated by swooping over the glistening waters, and within an instant caught a squiggling fish.

"Now you try it," he encouraged.

Roger, being quite a bit smaller than the eagle, swooped, saw a *tiny* wriggling form, and grabbed it with his back claws.

"Excellent," said Mel. "I have to take this one up to feed the lads, but why don't you try yours now?"

Roger nibbled a bit of the fish. He did not like it at all, and made a face to himself—he did not want to offend Mel. He gobbled it down anyway, as he was hungry.

"Want to go for another?" asked Mel.

"Oh, no thanks, that was quite enough," Roger hastily said. He was still hungry, but knew he could not face another fish.

"Alright then, let's head back to the nest."

Once back at the nest, Mel tore off strips of the fish, and fed it to Max and Billy. After eating, these two fell asleep right away ...

"Ok, that's done." Mel sighed. "You are pretty brave, for someone so young," Mel said to Roger. "Let's fly just a little further up; I want to show you something."

Roger cheerfully followed Mel even higher. Mel finally landed on a large branch, so high up Roger felt a wee bit dizzy.

"Look over there." Mel, with his beak, pointed to a shimmering meadow, which almost seemed suspended in air. "This is a magical place, which can only be found when one is ready to leave *this* world. All eagles go to the meadow, upon reaching the end of their time in this world. If *you* ever feel that you are ready to leave this world, which frankly I do not think you are a natural to, the meadow will be there."

"I've seen it," Roger said He remembered his dream of a meadow.

"You *are* magical then," Mel replied as the image faded away. "I *thought* so. We don't get many dragons in these woods; you're the first I've seen. I suspected you might be able to see the meadow. Not many of us can view it until we are ready to *go* there."

"I almost feel like I've been in the meadow before," Roger stammered. "Do you think my mother might be in the meadow? Did I come from there?"

"You know what, Roger? I think she may very well be in the meadow, and maybe you did come from there; so much is unknown. I *do* know that you should head home. The wind has died down somewhat, and even so, you are managing very well. Do you think you can make it back? I can carry you, if you like."

"No, thank you," replied Roger bravely. "I am certain I'll be fine."

Roger and Mel flew back down to the nest. Roger thanked his hosts profusely, bid his farewells, and headed back to the ridge.

Mel called out after him, "We may see you again! Take care!"

Roger was very thoughtful as he flew back to Sheila's yard. He was curious about his origins and even more so about the meadow—the one he had seen in his dreams, and just recently with Mel. Mel had told him that the meadow was magical and that he, Roger, was magical as well. Mel had also said that eagles were considered by many to be figures of mystery and magic, too.

"That is probably why I can see the meadow at times," Mel had explained.

Roger had enjoyed his visit with the eagles—not so much the fishing part—he much preferred pizza, chips, and warm blueberry muffins. He was just flying over the base of the ridge when he spotted his furry and feathered pack of dwarves. They were settled in a dense group of trees, near where Roger had been found. Roger swooped down immediately.

"Roger!" squawked Soot. "We thought you were a goner! We flew over to Sheila's yard to visit. You *weren't* in the greenhouse, that much we could see, but then, *then*, we saw you with the eagles!"

"How did you get out?" queried Jasper, before Roger had a chance to respond.

"I'm quite fine," Roger reassured his friends. He told them everything that had happened.

"I *knew* they were eagles, just like I somehow knew what all of you were. And after speaking with Mel I'm certain that I *am* a dragon."

"I don't think anyone can blame you for wanting to practice flying. You had no idea you would be caught up in a chinook," Jack said. "I am curious, however. Why are you so concerned about *what* you are? What is important is who you are. It *is* strange to meet a dragon, I must say. I *have* been told of them living in the distant past, and in the mea ..." Here Jack's voice trailed off.

"I could picture all of you in my head when you found me," Roger said in answer to Jack's question, "but I couldn't place myself."

"Give it time," encouraged Jasper. "You only just hatched, after all."

"I guess," Roger said doubtfully. He wondered if he should mention what Mel said about the meadow but decided to wait for another time.

"I should be getting back," he said.

"We can fly with you," volunteered Jack.

Roger, although he was certain he could find his way on his own, was happy for the company. Scrambling, hopping, and flying, they made their way back to Sheila's yard. Jasper remained discretely just outside the entrance to the neighborhood, along with Tip.

"Remember," he said to his friends, "humans are not fond of coyotes."

"And I won't be able to get into the yard," added Tip. "We'll wait here for you to come back."

"You are flying very well," commented Soot. "Your wings have gotten so much stronger in such a short period of time."

"You'll be able to come visit us," added Jack. "And when you're a little older, maybe you would like to come and live on the ridge."

Roger was not certain he wanted to live on the ridge, especially if it involved raw fish. He wisely said nothing; he did not want to offend his friends. At any rate, they were now in Sheila's yard, so he was spared a reply.

Roger wondered if he would be able to get back inside the greenhouse. He thought the chinook might have blown the door closed. He knew Sheila could open the door, but he was not sure he would be able to. Fortunately, he did not have to be concerned. The greenhouse door stood open. Sheila was inside calling his name.

"Roger! Roger? Where are you? Oh, I should have checked on him sooner!"

"I'd better go in," Roger told his friends. "Thank you for flying back with me."

"We'll see you later," Jack called. Once they had flown and scampered away, Roger flew into the greenhouse.

"Hi, Sheila," chirped Roger as he landed beneath the huge leaves of the philodendron.

"Roger! You scared me to death! Where have you been? How did you get out?"

"The door was open, and I wanted to stretch my wings. When I flew out, however, this great wind grabbed me, and I was blown away. An eagle found me and taught me how to fish …" Roger's voice trailed off when he realized that Sheila was staring at him with wide, alarmed eyes.

"You were with eagles, and they didn't eat you? Well, obviously not, I guess."

"No, in fact they were rather nice, and Mel showed me this … oh wait, what is that delicious smell?"

"That's pizza," Sheila replied. "I'll go grab you some now. I'll make certain I close the door properly this time."

Roger settled in his little nest, much relieved that Sheila had not scolded him for taking off (even though that had *not* been his intention). He was very hungry, and he liked pizza, so he contentedly waited for his dinner.

Chapter 6

Sheilas People

Mark and his friend Matthew had not been able to catch up with Sheila after she had snatched Roger away from the ridge. It was now the day after Roger had been found. Mark felt guilty that he had not gone looking for the little scaly guy right away, and he wondered where Sheila had hidden him. *He must be around here somewhere*, he thought. Mark decided to go search for Roger, after dinner of course. Mark was a healthy young boy, and he was hungry.

Gail, the housekeeper, called out, "Mark, dinner is ready." Gail had made pizza, one of Mark's favorites, with a large green salad. Happily, he tucked in to eat. Sheila was lying under the table, begging with woeful eyes.

"Now, Sheila," Mark scolded, "you've had your supper; no begging!"

Much to his surprise, Sheila snatched two pieces of pizza off the platter and went scurrying off, toenails sliding across the polished floor. She nudged open the doors to the backyard with her right paw and ran out. Mark started to go after her, but Gail stopped him.

"Finish your supper, Mark. I've got her," Gail said.

*****

"What are you doing, you silly dog?" Gail cried as she ran after Sheila. She was surprised to see Sheila going into the greenhouse. She was even more surprised when Sheila dropped the pizza under the leaves of the philodendron. *That dog is crazy*, Gail thought.

*****

Roger saw Sheila dash over to him. She quickly dropped the pizza at his feet, and then she dashed off again before he could even thank her. He wondered at her hurry but told himself that if she left the door open again, he would stay put. He was just munching on his first slice when he heard a strange voice:

"Oh, it's a lizard—an exotic one at that—one of those flying ones. I love lizards. I wonder why I didn't know about him. I wonder what he's been eating. I certainly hope there are not a lot of crickets hopping around in here—I haven't seen any, thank goodness. Would you look at that! The little guy likes pizza. I don't think I've ever heard of a pizza-eating lizard before. Mind you, my cat used to eat olives."

Roger looked up into sparkling brown eyes with his yellowish green eyes, half a piece of pizza still clasped in his front paw. Roger thought that this was probably Gail. He wondered if he should talk to her, considering what Sheila had said about many humans "not being able to see or hear anything unusual." *She can see me, at least,* he thought. He decided to introduce himself.

"I'm Roger," he squawked.

"Did you just speak to me?" asked the human, in surprise.

Roger was delighted; not only could this human see him, she could hear and understand him as well!

"I *did* speak to you. Are you Gail?"

"I am indeed," Gail replied after opening and closing her mouth several times. She reached out with one hand and gently touched Roger.

"You *are* real," she said. "How is it that you can talk?"

Roger was not entirely sure why Gail could understand him; he was simply delighted that she could.

"I think it's because I'm a dragon and somewhat magical. Sheila said that most people would probably not even see me, much less hear or understand me. Mark and Matthew could understand me, however. Sheila said that is probably because they are still young enough to be open to magic and the unusual. *You* must also believe in magic." Roger gazed at Gail with his beautiful jewel like eyes.

Gail shook her head and straightened up. Roger took that opportunity to finish his first slice of pizza and start on the second. Gail was watching him closely.

"Well, this is a strange day," she said. "I've met a talking, pizza-eating dragon. I *have* always believed in magic, Roger. I had so many imaginary friends as a young girl that my parents would joke about adding an addition to our house. Roger, you have obviously met the boys and Sheila as well. I can't wait to hear this story. Why don't we go inside, and then you can tell me how you came to be in the greenhouse? It looks like you could use another slice of pizza, too. I am very curious to hear what Mark has to say; he never mentioned you at all. Mind you, if I hadn't met you myself, I probably wouldn't have believed him."

Roger found himself being picked up, pizza and all, and carried out of the greenhouse. At first, he thought about protesting; his ridge-living friends would not know where he was. After further thought, he comforted himself by deciding his friends would probably not be looking for him again until the next day. He was also very curious to see what "inside" looked like, so he remained quiet and finished his pizza.

Roger saw Mark as Gail hurried into the kitchen, Sheila at his feet; both of them were staring at him. Mark's mouth was hanging open, and a slice of pizza dangled from his fingers.

"Roger!" Mark blurted. "Gail found you!"

"Yes," Gail replied before Roger could say anything. "I followed Sheila into the greenhouse and spotted this little winged lizard under the philodendron. Suddenly, Roger introduced himself; I just about fell over in shock. I've brought him in for more pizza and to tell us his story." Roger settled himself on a couple of cushions on a kitchen chair. Gail handed him another slice of pizza and told Roger that she was ready for him to describe his adventure.

Roger told Gail and Mark everything, including being reunited with his friends in the greenhouse. Roger, being a very wise little dragon, did *not* think that the time was right to describe his adventure with the chinook and meeting the eagles. He decided, quite correctly, that he had given Gail and Mark enough to chew on.

"So, that's where Sheila took you," Mark said, once Roger finished speaking. "I was going to look for you after supper."

"Speaking of supper," Gail said, "it looks like we're all finished—unless you would like another slice of pizza, Roger?"

"No thank you!"

"I'll clear up then. Roger, do you want to go with Mark to his room, or would you rather go back to the greenhouse? Frankly, I think you would be more comfortable in the house." Gail was quickly loading the dishwasher as she spoke.

Roger thought about his choices. He did prefer being inside over being in the greenhouse, and he was curious to see Mark's room. He was simply curious about everything. *Quite understandable*, he told himself. *I am newly hatched after all.*

"I would like to stay inside," Roger said shyly. "I just need to let my friends know where I am." Roger looked at Sheila as he said this.

"Oh, yes, I can tell them," Sheila said, understanding Roger's silent request.

That being settled, Roger rode in style to Mark's room on his shoulder.

"I don't think I should fly in here right now," Roger told Mark. "I *can* fly. It's just that this is like being in the greenhouse—there is not a great deal of room."

Roger was fascinated with Mark's boy cave. He settled himself on the corner of Mark's desk and looked around. This space was not at all like what he had been in before. He could not see any trees, bushes, birds, coyotes, or rabbits. What he saw were large, flat, shiny things with other shiny things placed before them.

"What are those?" he squawked.

"Oh, that's a flat-screen TV and a computer. Those are various games. I've got a Wii, an Xbox 360, PlayStation, and that's an iPhone," Mark replied.

"What do you need them for?"

"Well," Mark seemed to be at a loss for words, "I use the computer for school, and the rest are mainly for play. Here, I'll show you." Mark grabbed a couple of game controllers and passed one to Roger.

Roger watched as Mark made a bunch of little figures dance around one of the screens, simply by pressing buttons. Roger used the pad of one of his little clawed fingers on his controller and saw more figures appear.

"What are they doing?" he asked.

"They're trying to win several games to get to a trophy," Mark said. "Your guys are trying to get there first."

Roger found that he could move his figures around quite well, bu did not actually understand why he was trying to win a trophy, whate that was. He put his controller down, and Mark did as well.

"I'll show you the computer, Roger," Mark said. "Oh, wait! I shou phone Matthew. He'll want to know you're here, I'm sure." Mark grabbe the iPhone and asked someone—Matthew, Roger assumed—to com over.

Mark was showing the computer to Roger when thundering footsteps could be heard on the stairs. A boy's head peered around the doorway. Roger recognized Matthew from the ridge.

"Hi, Mark. Roger, it is good to see you! We were wondering where Sheila had taken you!"

"Sheila put me in the greenhouse," Roger told Matthew. He did not mention that Sheila had not wanted him to go to Matthew's house; he did not want to hurt the boy's feelings. Roger was not only a very wise little dragon; he was also very sensitive.

Matthew picked up the controller that Roger had discarded; he and Mark started to play the trophy-seeking game. Roger watched with interest; although he had no desire to play again himself, the brightly colored characters darting over the screen fascinated Roger. Finally, both boys put their controllers down; the game was over.

"I had better go home," Matthew said. "We *do* have school tomorrow."

"What is school?" Roger asked.

"It's where we go to learn stuff," Mark replied.

"Does everyone go?"

"Most *people* go to school," Mark answered awkwardly. "Animals seem to be born knowing stuff. Gail calls it a sixth sense."

Roger considered Mark's words and realized that he knew many things after being hatched that no one had told him. He was curious about this school, however, and decided that he wanted to see it.

"May I go with you, please?" he asked.

"I *guess* you can come with us," Mark replied. "You will have to stay outside. There are many trees around the school; you can hide in one of those. There is always activity in the yard, too; you will have people to watch.

"It will be kind of like watching you play your trophy game," Roger said happily, "except these are real people."

It was settled; Roger was going to school in the morning. For now, Roger and the two boys needed to get some sleep. Matthew went home. Mark climbed into his bed, and Roger snuggled on a cushion in a corner.

Before going to sleep, Roger was wondering about something.

"Do you not have a mum either?" he asked. "Is that why Gail looks after you and Sheila?"

"Yes, I have a mum and dad," Mark replied slowly. "They're away right now on a trip, with Matthew's mum and dad. Gail looks after us whenever they go away. Matthew has an older brother looking after him."

"I'm glad you have parents and Gail," said Roger sleepily. He settled into a very pleasant dream.

Chapter 7

Roger Goes to School

The next morning, Roger woke up to see Mark bustling around his room.

"Ready to go, Roger? I've made room for you in my backpack."

Roger scrambled off his cushion and flew to the top of Mark's backpack. He squeezed himself inside; it was a tight fit but secure. Once Roger was nestled in the backpack, Mark handed him a muffin. Roger was delighted to find that it was blueberry. Mark thrust his arms through the pack's straps and flew upstairs and out of the house. Mark grabbed a bike, and Roger felt himself jostled a little as Mark rode the bike away from the house.

Matthew was on his own bike, waiting for them.

"You okay, Roger?" called Matthew.

"Yupf," Roger replied in a garbled fashion; his mouth was full of muffin.

The three rode off to school. The school was about five blocks away. It was nestled against two other schools in another pleasant residential area in Varsity. Hence, it only took about five minutes for them to get there, including crossing the one busy road. The boys locked their bikes in the rack, and swung their packs off their backs. Roger was gazing curiously out of Mark's pack. His head was turning this way and that way.

There were a lot of humans wandering around. There was a solid-looking building, which Mark told him was the school. There was a structure that humans were climbing on, which he was told was a jungle gym, and a large expanse of grass, which was the schoolyard. At the end of this expanse, there were several trees clustered together.

"Roger, those are the trees I was telling you about," Mark said. "You can watch the playground, visit with whichever birds stop by, snooze. All of the trees are very leafy and have lots of flowers, so you should be well hidden."

Both boys ran over to the trees, and Roger climbed out of Mark's backpack to settle himself within the fragrant bower. Roger was given a large bag of potato chips, a sack containing three apples, and a large plastic water bottle. Matthew tied these to a limb of the tree.

Roger had little difficulty with the water bottle—he was clever with his claws—and he sampled an apple. He liked it, too. *Actually,* Roger thought to himself, *I've liked everything I've been given to eat. I think pizza is still my favorite, though.*

"Now, Roger," cautioned Mark, "it is very important that you stay put, okay?"

"Okay," replied Roger. He was quite comfortable. He was nestled into a kind of natural basket made by overlapping branches of the tree. He had food and water and could watch the humans running around on the field. Roger was also fond of sleep and thought he might just nap.

"We'll be in there most of the day," Mark pointed to the school, "but we'll come and check on you at lunchtime. We really won't have time at recess, but you may see us."

The bell rang with a loud clang, and both boys ran back to the school. Roger finished his apple, including the core, and snoozed for a bit. He was brought abruptly awake by a cawing in his ear; it was Soot, the crow. Patch and Jack were dispersed among the branches as well.

"Hi," Roger chirped happily. "What are you guys doing here?"

"Soot and I were flying to Sheila's house, and we saw you take off with Mark," Jack replied. "We decided to follow you."

Roger was delighted. He had wondered what he was going to do all day; there had not really been a great deal of activity in the schoolyard. He was happy that he had been allowed to go to school with the boys that morning, but he had expected a bit more adventure.

Roger glanced down and saw Tip nibbling away, but he did not see Jasper.

"Where is Jasper?" Roger asked, before he remembered that Jasper stayed away from humans. "Never mind. I guess he's on the ridge?"

"He is there," Jack replied. "Would you like to visit him?

"Well, I don't know if I should," Roger replied uncertainly. "I would like to visit him, but I told the boys I would stay put. And what if someone sees me? I haven't seen anyone else like me around."

"We'll have you back before the boys know that you're gone," Jack assured him.

"You can fly with us," added Soot. "We'll go together, and you'll blend right in."

"Come on, Roger," urged Soot. "Jasper would like to see you again, and you'll get more wing practice!"

Roger needed no additional encouragement. He would dearly love to go to the ridge. He was delighted to be in the company of his new friends and looking forward to seeing the crusty old Jasper.

"Let's go," he cried, and they all swooped off toward the ridge.

Jasper was hidden close to the cliffs under a bush.

"Hello, Roger," said Jasper as Roger landed at his feet. "I'm glad to see you, and I can't wait to hear about what you've been doing. We will have more privacy further down the cliff; let's head along this way. Tip and Patch will come with me. Jack, you lead the lads through the branches. We'll meet down by the river, in the woods."

The ridge embraced more gentle slopes than the harsh, unforgiving cliffs. It was down such a slope that Jasper led Roger and his friends. It was a path within the woods that ran beside the human path. The river trilled and wove her way gently, gently, below this passage.

Roger followed Jack and Soot to a clearing near the river. He was once again transported. A theatre unfolded before him, an ancient stage—a cathedral challenging man's best-made works. Roger was enchanted; he simply listened to the chorus ringing around him.

Suddenly, a great swoosh of wings interrupted Roger's daydream. He watched in awe as a large bald eagle landed on the ground several feet away.

"Mel!" cried Roger happily. "Hey, guys, it's Mel!" Roger looked around for his other friends but saw that they had, for some reason, moved away.

"Hi, Roger," Mel said. "I was on fishing duty and saw you down here, so I thought I'd quickly pop by to say hello and to see how you're doing. Mildred will want to hear about you as well. Are your friends treating you all right?"

"Oh yes, very well," Roger replied enthusiastically. "I am staying with my boy, Mark."

"You're staying with humans. That is interesting. How did you get *here?*"

"Well, my boy and his friend took me to school with them. I was sleeping in a tree when some of my friends found me. We decided to come to the ridge to visit with Jasper, who does not leave the ridge often." Roger pointed at the coyote.

"It seems to me like you are in good hands. If you ever need anything or just want to come for a visit, you know where we are. I suppose I should take off; it's getting late for lunch." Mel bowed to Roger and swept away.

"Oh it's lunchtime!" Roger exclaimed. He suddenly remembered that the boys had said something about checking on him at lunch. "I better fly back. The boys will be looking for me!"

"Jack and I will fly back with you," said Soot.

The threesome returned to the school. Roger scooted himself back in the tree and grabbed another apple from the sack.

"We'll take off then, Roger," Jack said, "but we're around Sheila's yard. We'll watch out for you!" With that, the two birds flew off.

While munching on his apple, Roger peered out cautiously through the tree branches to see what was going on in the schoolyard. The yard was deserted. Roger guessed, correctly, that he had missed lunch hour.

I'll just have a nap, he said to himself. He finished the apple and went to sleep.

Roger slept until he heard the sounds of humans running around; it was afternoon recess. Roger peered out again to scan the schoolyard, but he could see neither Mark nor Matthew. There were many other young humans to watch, however. Roger was highly entertained by the sight of balls being chased and limbs scrambling up the jungle gym. A loud clanging of a bell interrupted his amusement. Everyone scrambled back inside the school, followed by a loud bang of the shutting door. Sighing, Roger settled back into his nest to wait.

Sometime later, the bell rang again, and Roger was jerked awake (yes, he had decided to nap again). Humans streamed out of the school, but they seemed to be leaving the schoolyard.

Oh, I bet the boys are coming now, he thought.

He peered out again and was certain he saw Mark getting on a strange yellow contraption (a school bus). He forgot his warning to stay put (again), and he forgot that Mark had not arrived in such a thing. He was simply determined to follow the boy whom he thought was Mark. Roger took off and flew after the boy into the bus, landing on one of the empty seats. The bus doors closed. The bus rattled away from the school.

"Did you see something fly in here?" Roger heard one child say.

"What would fly in the bus?" another child scoffed in reply.

Roger breathed a sigh of relief. He was glad that he had not been seen. His relief was short lived however when he realized that the boy he followed was not in fact Mark.

The boy *looked* similar—from the back anyway. He also realized that he couldn't fly back outside; he was trapped. Roger was more than a little frightened. He pulled his wings around him and tried to make himself as small as possible. Eventually, the bus rolled to a halt. Roger waited until the children had exited. Then he flung himself out the doors, wings beating frantically.

Roger flew around aimlessly, not caring if anyone saw him; he was so scared and lonely. He was finally so tired he flew into a shady tree. It was in the yard of a large house with a beautiful lawn that backed onto a natural park. The surroundings reminded him of the ridge, but he knew it was not.

"Who are you?" a gruff voice demanded from beneath him. Roger glanced down into the deep brown eyes of a large brown and black dog; it was clearly not a coyote. Nor did he resemble Sheila.

"I'm Roger," the little dragon replied in a quivering voice.

"Bear," barked the dog, "and this is Kobe." Another dog was sprawled beside Bear. This dog was more slender than Bear but had the same coloring. His jaw was a bit longer than Bear's, and his ears stuck up, whereas Bear's ears flopped down.

"Come down from there so we can see you better," Bear requested.

Roger, quite tentatively, flew down. He was not quite sure what to make of Kobe and Bear. Bear hankered over immediately and sniffed loudly at Roger. Roger, surprised, stepped back a few paces.

"Sorry!" Bear said. "I didn't mean to be rude. It's just how I get to know someone."

The other dog, Kobe, rose rather unsteadily to his feet and approached Roger. Kobe also sniffed Roger but in a much more gentle fashion.

"Hello, Roger," Kobe said. "We haven't seen the likes of you around here before."

Suddenly, Kobe's legs seemed to fold beneath him. Roger observed this action with considerable alarm.

"Are you okay?" Roger asked.

"I'm not very steady on my feet anymore," Kobe replied apologetically. "I can't walk or run as well as I used to either."

"Why not?" blurted Roger, and almost immediately wished he had not spoken. Kobe did not seem to take offense, however, much to Roger's relief.

"I'm not entirely sure," Kobe replied slowly. "I have heard my people talk about something called Wobbly Leg Syndrome. I don't know anything about it except that it apparently affects my back; I guess that is why I'm so clumsy. I had to go away for a while to have what my people called an operation. I think it was to help my back."

Roger was hanging on to Kobe's every word. He found himself feeling dreadfully sorry for him. The big, beautiful dog seemed to be perfectly at ease; however, there was only a shadow hinting of sadness in his huge brown eyes.

"Enough about me," Kobe said, breaking into Roger's thoughts. "Tell us your story, Roger."

Roger told the dogs every detail: his realization that he was a dragon and hence somewhat magical; his adventure with the chinook and the eagles; his moving into Mark's house. Roger did not mention the meadow; he wanted to keep this knowledge to himself for a little while longer. He didn't really know how to describe it, anyway.

"A *dragon*," said Kobe, awestruck. "No wonder we haven't seen anyone like you before."

"Coyote?" both dogs exclaimed.

"Eagles?" they added.

"And now you're lost," Bear commented.

"Yes," sighed Roger. "I should have listened to Mark, but I wanted to see the ridge and Jasper. I saw Mel, too. I'm going to try to find my way home." Roger prepared to fly off.

"Wait," Bear said. "I know where the ridge is. Our human sometimes takes us down there to run, as a change from our park. He always takes us toward those big rocks, which are called mountains. Try flying toward the mountains, and I'm sure you'll see your ridge."

"Thank you!" said Roger, much relieved.

"Good luck," both dogs sincerely told him. "It's been interesting meeting you!"

Roger took to flight once again and now had a general sense of where to fly, thanks to Bear's instructions. He took off in that direction, looking down periodically to check his environment.

Well, Roger thought he was the luckiest dragon in the world. As he glanced down, there was Mark! It *was* Mark this time; he was sure of it! Mark's friend Matthew was there, too, along with another boy Roger did not know. Roger was unconcerned about the unknown boy. Mark obviously knew him, and that was good enough for Roger. Down he flew, landing none too gracefully at the boys' feet.

"Hi," he gasped, rather breathlessly.

The other boy stared down at Roger with a baffled expression.

"What is that?" he queried.

"I'm Roger. I am a dragon."

"Roger!" cried Mark. "Am I ever we glad to see you!"

"We looked for you at lunch and after school," Matthew added.

"We couldn't stay for long after school. We had to come to Steve's to finish a project for science," Mark explained apologetically. "Steve's been away, and today was the only day we had to meet. We were going to look for you again on our way home."

The new boy, Steve, was muttering to himself. "Talking dragons?"

Mark suggested that they go inside. "I'll explain once we're in the house," Mark said.

Roger allowed himself to be scooped up; he was rather tired from all of his flying, and he was getting hungry. Much to his delight, once they were inside Steve's house, (which was very much like Mark's, Roger noted), chips and apples were given.

"Do you like those?" Steve asked Roger, after passing out the snacks.

"I do, very much," Roger replied. "Thank you, Steve."

Mark told Steve about Roger's arrival at his home and then turned to Roger.

"Where did you go?" Mark asked the little dragon.

Roger told the boys about his adventures that afternoon.

"I'm sorry I flew off," Roger said, once he finished his story. "I didn't mean to worry anyone."

"We're just glad you're back with us," Mark replied. "Now we'd better finish that science project. I wish it were a biology project, Roger. You could have been the star."

Once the work was complete, Roger happily tucked himself back into Mark's backpack for the journey home. He hoped there would be pizza for supper again that evening, but he was so hungry he decided he would even eat—shudder—fish.

Matthew wheeled off to his own house.

When they arrived home, Mark and Roger (on Mark's shoulder) headed toward the kitchen, from which a delicious fragrance floated, teasing Roger's nostrils.

"Roger," Mark said, stopping at the kitchen entrance, "it might be best not to mention your adventure."

Roger, who had been thinking the same thing, readily agreed.

"Oh yay, tacos," Mark murmured as he and Roger sat down. "You'll like these, Roger. Gail makes her own tortillas."

Roger told Gail a little bit about his day at school as she dished out the tacos. (He left out the bits about getting lost and meeting the dogs).

These tacos are very good, he thought.

After dinner, Roger settled on his cushion in Mark's room and promptly fell asleep. He was a very tired dragon; he had a busy day, and his tummy was comfortably full. He dreamt of two large dogs playfully chasing him in a huge field full of flowers.

Chapter 8

Jasper Is Stranded

Tuesday brought sunshine and blue skies; a beautiful day was in the making.

Before heading in to breakfast, Mark and Roger discussed what Roger should do on this glorious day.

"I don't think I want to go back to school today," Roger admitted.

"You can stay here with Sheila, in the backyard," Mark said. "I'll get some snacks together for you."

"That would be great," enthused Roger. He hoped his ridge buddies would pop by for a visit.

Gail was in the kitchen preparing pancakes.

"Are you going to school again, Roger?" she asked.

"No," Roger replied, "I thought I would stay outside with Sheila if that's okay."

"That sounds like a good idea; it's supposed to be a nice day. You can visit with Sheila, and if you become sleepy, you can always curl up in the doghouse. It is a very comfortable doghouse. I will not be around very much today, as I have errands to run. I'll just get some snacks together, Roger, and you should be fine until I get home."

"Already on it," Mark told Gail. He held up a plastic bag containing apples, chips, granola bars, and water.

"Good. We should be all set then," Gail said. "I'll be off. I will see you both later." Gail sailed out of the kitchen.

Roger followed Mark into the backyard. Mark set the bag of snacks under a shady tree.

"I'd better go now. I don't want to be late," he told Roger. Mark patted Sheila on the head.

"You look after Roger," Mark said, and he left the yard.

Roger settled himself next to Sheila, who had been snoozing under a tree. She sat up as Roger arrived.

"I didn't get much of a chance to talk to you yesterday," Sheila said. "I know you went to school with Mark. I also know that you flew to the ridge."

"How did you know that?" Roger asked, surprised.

"Your friends stopped by the yard yesterday afternoon; they told me. Jack also mentioned that he and Soot flew back to the school a bit later, and you were not there. Where did you go?"

Before Roger could reply, he heard a rustling in the tree above his head. Soot, Jack, and Patch appeared on one of the many branches.

"Your friends flew back here when they could not find you at the school," Sheila explained. "We were all worried about you. I asked them to come by again today. You are obviously okay, but we'd like to hear what happened."

Roger watched in amazement as Sheila then trotted to the back gate, stood on her hind legs, and pushed up the latch with her snout. She shoved the gate open, and Tip hopped in.

"Good thing the gate wasn't locked," Sheila told Roger, "or I would not have been able to do that."

"I'm glad to see everyone," Roger stammered, "but I didn't think Tip was allowed in your yard."

"I'm making an exception," Sheila said. "As I said, everyone was very worried about you. Your feathered friends asked if it was possible that Tip join us."

"I promised not to eat any shrubs," Tip said to Roger.

The group gathered around Roger, who was gaping at them with mixed happiness and uncertainty. He sensed tension of some sort. They were all looking at him.

"What?" he finally stammered.

"The group has asked Jack to speak for them," Sheila continued. "Jack, you're on."

"Roger," Jack began, "I know Soot and I dropped you off safely back at the school yesterday, and we said we would watch out for you around Sheila's yard. Well, we flew back to the ridge, and after some discussion, the group decided that Soot and I should fly by the school, once again, just to check on you."

"We didn't take very good care of you after we first found you," Tip interrupted, "and we did not want to repeat our mistake."

"Yes," Jack continued, "as Tip said, we decided to take some extra care—you were alone in that tree. When Soot and I returned to the school and couldn't find you, we were worried sick."

"Oh …" Roger stammered, feeling guilty. Glancing around, he could instantly tell that "oh" was not going to be enough.

"Where did you go?" asked Tip.

"I guess I was late getting back to the school because the boys, who said they were going to come by, did not show up," Roger said. "There were other humans in the schoolyard later, but I didn't see the boys. I was starting to feel scared. I mainly slept and ate, so it wasn't too bad. I heard a bell, and all of these humans started leaving the schoolyard. I thought I saw Mark get on a bus—Mark told me that it was a bus later—so I flew in after him. I didn't know you were going to come back."

"You are a daft lizard," scolded Jack. "You told us that you rode to the school with Mark on his *bike*. If you didn't arrive at school on a bus, why would you leave on one?" Jack shook his blue and white feathery head. "Tell us what happened next."

Roger reported meeting Kobe and Bear, the descriptions of whom prompted Sheila to comment, "I've seen two large dogs fitting those descriptions on the ridge; they've never introduced themselves, and I'm not allowed to approach them. They are a Doberman and a Rottweiler." There was a collective shudder from the group.

"They're very nice. I'm sure you'd like them, Sheila. Bear was quite kind; he told me how to get home. Kobe has something wrong with his legs; he had trouble standing and didn't walk like Bear, or like you or Jasper," Roger said. "He's also very nice, but he did seem a little bit sad."

"He used to run like the wind." Sheila sighed. "Poor Kobe."

Jack cleared his throat. "So Bear showed you how to get home …"

"Yes," Roger replied, "he said he knew that when his human took them to the ridge, they went toward the mountains. Bear told me to fly that way and keep checking down."

"And you followed his instructions and found the ridge?" Jack further prompted. "I'm surprised we didn't see you."

"No, I didn't make it to the ridge," Roger replied. "I found the boys and one of their friends. I looked down, and there they were."

"That is quite the story, Roger." Jack again shook his blue and white head.

"I didn't mean to worry anyone," Roger said in a small voice.

"Mark told me to look after you," Sheila announced, "and that is what I'm going to do. No taking off today. Okay, Roger?"

"We'll hang around to visit for a while, lad," said Soot.

"Tip!" barked Sheila suddenly. Tip was slyly sniffing around some bushes. "Get out!"

"Sorry, Sheila. I am a rabbit, after all," Tip replied apologetically. "It's in my nature to nibble on plants. Thanks for letting me sit in on the meeting. I'll say good-bye for now, and I'm going to hop down to the ridge and tell Jasper the story."

Sheila let Tip out and quickly latched the gate.

"I could use a lie down," Sheila announced. "That was mentally exhausting."

Sheila climbed into her doghouse and, Roger, following, turned back to his friends. Suddenly, they took to the trees with a flurry of wings and a scampering of paws. The patio doors slid open, and Gail appeared on the deck.

"Roger, do you know where Sheila is?" Gail asked. "I can't believe it! I completely forgot that she has an appointment with her veterinarian. Goodness, I must be getting old!"

"Sheila is in her doghouse," Roger replied just as the lab reappeared. Gail produced a leash, and Sheila rolled her eyes at Roger.

"I was really hoping she wouldn't remember," Sheila told Roger. "I don't know how long we'll be gone. You will be here when we get home?"

"Yes," Roger replied firmly.

"Let's go, Sheila," Gail cooed. "Roger, I am going to take Sheila with me after her appointment for the remainder of my errands. The afternoon looks beautiful, so you should be fine. And you can always snuggle in the doghouse, unless—do you want to go inside?"

"No, thank you," Roger replied. "Most of my ridge friends are here. I will visit with them."

Once Gail and Sheila left, the feathery twosome and Patch flew and scrambled back into the yard.

"So," drawled Soot slowly, "Sheila's gone for a while. Want to fly quickly down to the ridge and visit with Jasper?"

Roger, who would like nothing better, perked up but then shook his scaly little head. "Best not." He sighed. "I got into enough trouble at the school."

"Whatever are you thinking, Soot? We almost lost Roger yesterday!" Jack scolded. "And we were flying all over looking for him."

"And my paws are sore from all the tree hopping I had to do," whined Patch.

"But we'll be with him," Soot argued. "We'll fly down, say a quick hello to Jasper, then fly right back here. Patch, you don't have to come with us."

"I'd really like to say hello to Jasper—and if we come right back?" Roger's voice trailed off, and he looked in a mournful manner at Jack, Soot, and Patch. There was a collective sigh from Jack and Patch.

"Okay, there should be no harm done if we're quick." Jack finally said, "Patch, are you coming with us or not?"

"I think I'll hang around the bird feeder," Patch said. "See you later! Say hi to Jasper." With that, Patch scurried up a tree and onto the branch from which the bird feeder hung.

"Let's go, then," Jack called, and as he soared upward, the others followed. Jasper was not in his usual spot on the ridge. They did however see Tip, who was delicately munching on some bushes when they arrived. After exchanging greetings, Roger asked about Jasper.

"Have you seen him?" asked Roger. "I was going to stay with Sheila in her yard, but she had to go out. I decided it would be okay if I flew over for a quick hello and then went back."

"No, I'm sorry. I haven't seen him," Tip replied thoughtfully. "Wait a minute, he may be fishing. Yesterday he mentioned something about being tired of leaves and berries."

"It won't take long to fly down to the river," said Soot. "Roger, why don't we just quickly see if he's there, and if not, we can fly with you back to Sheila's yard."

The others agreed, and they soared down to the river. Jasper was initially nowhere to be seen. Suddenly, Roger spotted the coyote clinging to a log in the river, which was swirling angrily around him. From the shore, Roger detected the coyote's faint cries for help.

"Jasper's in trouble!" Roger exclaimed. "Will the two of you please fly over to him and tell him to hang on! I'll get the eagles; maybe they'll know what we can do to rescue him!"

"I'll go with you, Roger," Jack offered. "I think we may need the help of both eagles. You told us they had little ones; they'll need someone to stay with them while one of us takes them to Jasper."

Soot flew off swiftly to where Jasper was stranded. Roger and Jack took off to the lofty domain of the eagles. Roger was relieved to see that both of the adults were in the nest, along with their sleeping young.

"Why, Roger, it's good to see you, but whatever are you doing out in this storm? Oh, and who is your friend?" asked Mildred.

Roger noticed that it had started to rain—very hard. He was not concerned with the rain, however.

"This is Jack. Jack, this is Mildred, Mel, and those are their little ones. We need your help, if you can!"

Both eagles were now giving Roger their full attention.

"What's wrong?" urged Mel.

"Our friend Jasper is stuck on a log in the river. We're afraid he's going to drown! Is there any way to save him?" Roger looked at Mel anxiously.

"I think there is a way we can help," Mel replied. "We have to hurry; the river is very high with all the rain we've been having. It is extremely dangerous!"

"I'll stay with the boys since they know me," Roger said. "Jack can take you to where Jasper is."

"Thank you, Roger. We must hurry!" Mel said again. The three flew rapidly to the river.

Chapter 9

Jasper's Rescue

Roger waited anxiously for the birds to return. *What if nothing can be done?* he thought. He shuddered at the idea of crusty, independent Jasper trapped in the ruthless waves. He thought of the meadow and hoped Jasper was not ready to leave for it just yet.

It seemed a very long wait, but finally he saw the three coming back. Mel and Mildred popped into the nest, and Jack perched on the edge.

"Is Jasper okay?" asked Roger in a quivering voice.

"Yes he is, thanks to Mel and Mildred here. They were great!" Jack cried.

"Oh, thank you! Thank you! How did you save him?" Roger asked. He was curious now that he was no longer frightened out of his little dragon wits.

"He was in a great deal of trouble: I don't think he could have held on much longer," Mel told Roger. "We quickly decided what we could try. We flew to either side of the log, and each of us dug our claws into the wood. We flapped our wings and pulled the log through the water. We towed it up to a stable part of the riverbank."

"It was frightening," Mildred added. "The river is very powerful right now."

"I thought all three of us might be seeing the meadow very soon," Mel whispered to Roger.

"Jasper is cold, wet, and had a bad scare, but he's okay," Mildred said. "Speaking of your friend, you should go check on him. He would probably like to tell his story about how he arrived in the river himself."

"Thank you for staying with the boys," Mel said to Roger. "I hope we'll be seeing you again soon."

On that note, Roger and Jack flew back down, and Jack showed Roger where Jasper was waiting. The rain had stopped, but Jasper was still wet and cold.

"You saved my life! Thank you!" Jasper said as soon as he saw them. "If you had not spotted me and gone to get the eagles, I would have been lost."

"I'm just glad you're all right," Roger said. "How did you get out in the river?"

"I was looking for fish," Jasper replied. "I wandered further along the bank than I normally do, because the water was muddy and choppy. My regular fishing spots were hidden by the muddy water. I was hungry and grumpy, so I didn't notice the storm coming. The rain started to come down very hard.

"I was just standing on a log on the bank staring sadly at the churning water. *Guess it will be berries again*, I thought to myself. Suddenly there was a crash of thunder, and almost at the same time, the river spilled over its banks; the log upon which I had been standing was now in the roaring river. I frantically clung to the log with my claws. Soot did tell me that you had gone for help, but I didn't have much hope."

Jasper paused for a minute before continuing. "Suddenly I looked up and saw Jack and the two enormous eagles swooping toward me. I was never so glad to see anyone. They tugged the log to a safe spot where I could hop off."

"You must have been terrified," Roger said sympathetically.

"I was very scared," Jasper admitted. "I thanked both eagles over and over again. They were very gracious. When I asked them what I could do to thank them, they just said to get to higher ground.

"That was a close one," Jasper added. "I've never seen the river like that; one minute I was on the ground, and then not. I wanted to wait for both of you so I could thank you. But now I'm going to grab some berries and head back to my den to sleep." Jasper took his leave.

Roger, now that his scare was over and his friend was safe, realized that he was quite hungry as well. He would not say no to a nap either. He also realized that he had been away longer than he expected.

"I'd better fly back," he said to his friends (Soot had rejoined the group). "If Sheila's home, she will be worried and probably cross with me."

"Do you want us to fly with you?" asked Jack.

"No thank you," Roger said. "I'm sure I can make it back on my own. I'm going to curl up in Sheila's doghouse for a nap and a snack as soon as I'm home. No more adventure for me, not for today anyway."

"A snack does sound good," Jack said. After Roger reassured them he could get home safely, the birds went searching for their own snacks.

Roger flew home quickly. Sheila did not appear to be home yet. (The sun had come back out, and it was quite warm, so he was certain she would be outside if she was back.) He was a relieved dragon, as he grabbed a snack and crawled into Sheila's doghouse to munch and snooze.

Sheila crawled into the doghouse sometime later and Roger woke up.

"Hello, Roger," she said. "What did you do all day?"

"I ate and slept most of the time," Roger replied innocently, and he went back to sleep.

Chapter 10

Roger Is Advised of a Move

T he next couple of days passed uneventfully. Roger had been shaken by Jasper's near call, and he didn't want any new adventures for a while. He stayed in Sheila's yard and visited with his friends. He would fly into Matthew's yard on occasion to visit with Tip; Tip was forever next door. He did not fly back to the ridge to see Jasper or the eagles. The others told him that Jasper was fine and staying well away from the still swollen river.

One afternoon, Mark told Roger that he was finished with school for the summer.

"Two months of freedom, Roger!" he exclaimed. "Matthew and Steve are coming for supper to celebrate! Gail said she's making pizza!"

Everyone enjoyed the pizza—prepared with Gail's usual flair—but Roger noticed that Gail seemed troubled. Finally, after the pizza was devoured, Gail revealed what had been upsetting her.

"I have an announcement," she said. "It was supposed to be a nice surprise for Mark, to celebrate the end of the school year. A few weeks ago, I made plans to take Mark to visit my sister for a week; she lives in Edmonton. We are going to stay with her for a few days and at West Edmonton Mall for the remainder of the time."

"Wow!" all the boys cried.

"What's West Edmonton Mall?" asked Roger.

"The point is," Gail continued, waving away Roger's question, "I did not know Roger at that time. We cannot take either Roger or Sheila with us; my sister's place does not allow pets, nor does the hotel in West

Edmonton Mall—it's kind of like a huge playground for kids and adults, Roger."

"Oh" was the collective reply from Roger and the boys.

"I made arrangements for Sheila to stay with her veterinarian—they enjoy having her—but I didn't know about you, Roger. I do not know what to do. Everything is paid for. I've been trying to think of where you could stay."

Roger's heart went out to Gail, because she was upset.

"I suppose I could stay with my friends on the ridge," Roger suggested bravely, his heart pounding. He enjoyed visiting with his ridge friends in the yard or on the occasional flight to the ridge, but he didn't want to *live* there. He was almost certain that there wouldn't be pizza or muffins on the ridge.

"Oh, no, no," Gail told him, to his secret relief. "Going to live on the ridge is out of the question. Where would you sleep? What would you eat? I did come up with a couple of solutions. My first thought was that you could stay with Sheila's veterinarian. This is not a great idea, Roger, because you would have to stay in a small space—a kennel—and would not be able to fly. I very much prefer my other idea, which is why I wanted all of you here at the same time. Roger, you could go stay with Matthew or Steve while we're gone, if you'd like."

"I would like to go stay with Steve or Matthew, if possible." Roger shone his crystal-like eyes on the two boys.

"I wouldn't be able to take you, Roger," Steve said apologetically. "I'm going camping for two weeks."

"You'll come and stay with me, Roger," said Matthew.

"That would be great!" Roger replied. "Thank you, Matthew."

"Yes, thank you, Matthew," Gail repeated. "I really didn't like the idea of you going to the veterinarian's, Roger. Sheila will be able to run around with their dogs, but as I mentioned, you would have had to stay in a kennel. Now, Roger, why don't you go outside with Sheila. The boys and I will clean up."

"What about Sugar?" Mark asked in an anxious voice.

"She has actually been nice lately," Matthew replied. "I'll keep a close eye on her."

Roger wondered who Sugar was and was about to ask when Sheila motioned for him to follow her outside. Roger then remembered that Sheila had told him it was not safe at Matthew's house. He wondered if it had anything to do with the mysterious Sugar.

"Who is Sugar?" Roger asked, once they were outside. "Is she the reason you told me it was not safe at Matthew's house?"

"Sugar is Matthew's cat," replied Sheila. "I've never met her; she never goes outside. I have heard Mark talking about her to Gail. Apparently, she has attacked visitors, including Mark, and sometimes even Matthew and his family. I heard Mark say that Sugar has even been locked up in Matthew's downstairs family room at times. So, yes, in answer to your second question, that is why I said it was not "safe at Matthew's.""

"I could just go to the ridge, I guess," Roger said thoughtfully and somewhat sadly.

"No!" cried Sheila. "You heard what Gail said. If you're worried about Sugar, you can stay at the veterinarians. You would not be able to go outside and would not be able to see me or any of your other friends. It is only for a week though."

"I would much rather stay with Matthew," Roger said. "Matthew said Sugar's nice now and that he would keep an eye on her."

"And as I said, Roger, I've never met her," Sheila said. "Sometimes stories are stretched a bit, like balloons with too much air. I never should have said anything about Matthew's place not being safe, without having met Sugar. I should not have reached a conclusion based on what I heard. Maybe she is a little wacky, maybe not—but you can fly, Roger."

"You're right," Roger replied, much cheered up. "I'm sure it will be fine."

"What will be fine?" asked Jack, startling Roger. He had not noticed that Jack was in the yard. He looked up to see Jack perched on the overhead branch.

"I came for a visit and accidentally heard a bit of what sounded like an interesting conversation," Jack continued. "I'm sorry—I didn't mean to interrupt."

"Hi," Roger said. "Sheila and I were just discussing my move to Matthew's house for a week."

"What? Why is that happening?" Jack squawked and flew to the ground. "Roger, you can't do that! Patch and Soot, get down here!"

Roger's other two friends flew and climbed down from the leafy bower above.

"Hi, Roger, Sheila," Patch and Soot said together. "What's going on?"

"We have a problem," said Jack. "Roger is going to Matthew's house for a week!"

"Roger, why is *that* happening?" asked Patch, unknowingly copying Jack.

"Mark and Gail are going away for a week, and I can't go with them. I have nowhere else to go," Roger replied.

"Well, that's just silly," spluttered Jack. "You can stay on the ridge with us."

Roger did not want to hurt his friends' feelings, but he decided he should be honest with them. "I know I hatched on the ridge. I just don't think I want to live there." Roger looked at his friends apologetically.

"Do you *know* about Sugar?" asked Jack.

"Sheila told me a little bit she overheard from conversations between Mark and Gail," Roger replied. "She also said that she had not met Sugar, so she does not really know if what she heard is truth or just a tall tale. I thought about it and decided that I'm not going to worry about Sugar. I've liked everyone else I've met so far."

"Sugar does not come outside, so the three of us have never met her either," Jack admitted. "She just seems different. Sometimes, if she is by the glass door and sees us out in the yard, she goes crazy. She starts throwing herself at the door, and we can hear her howling; it can be quite unnerving."

"Matthew said that Sugar has been better and that he would watch her," Roger said bravely.

"You do seem to be very content staying with Sheila and Mark," Jack said. "And it can be harsh living on the ridge."

"I'll probably be outside most of the time, anyway," Roger added.

"It *is* only for a short time," stated Soot thoughtfully. "And it will be much the same as it is now; we'll come here, or you can fly to the ridge."

"And you can always fly over to this yard," Sheila pointed out.

With that, the group split up. Jack, Patch, and Soot headed back to the ridge. Sheila barked at the french doors, and Gail let Sheila and Roger back inside the house. Once inside, Roger noticed that several of Sheila's belongings were assembled in a large box. He looked at Gail inquiringly.

"Roger," Gail began, "I was going to take Sheila to the veterinarian's this evening, even though we are not leaving until tomorrow. Before we go, are you certain you want to stay with Matthew? I am sorry. I had forgotten about Sugar until Mark mentioned her after dinner."

"I will probably be outside most of the time." Roger repeated what he had told his friends. "I trust Matthew to look after me. Besides, I can fly away from her." Roger threw a quick glance at Sheila as he said this.

"Okay," Gail said, "if you are sure. We can always make another trip to the veterinarian's before we leave tomorrow, if you change your mind." Gail called for Mark to carry Sheila's box out to the car and attached a leash to Sheila's collar.

"Bye, Roger," Sheila called as she was led out. "See you in a week."

The remainder of the evening was quiet. After arriving home, Gail went into the kitchen to make muffins.

"These are for you and Matthew to take with you tomorrow," she told Roger, much to his delight.

Roger and Mark went to their room.

"I had better pack," Mark said. Roger watched curiously as Mark threw clothing into a large duffel bag, seemingly at random. Once this task was complete, dragon and boy curled up in their cozy beds.

I wonder what Sugar is like, Roger thought sleepily as he was drifting off. His dreams that night were of a pretty, white cat staring at him intently through a glass door.

Chapter 11

Roger Meets Sugar
(Crazy White Cat)

Roger woke the next morning feeling somewhat uneasy. He wondered why, until he remembered—oh yes, today was the day he would meet Sugar. "It will be interesting," he told himself.

Breakfast was toasted bagels and smoked salmon cream cheese. This was one of Roger's favorite breakfasts—it wasn't raw fish. He happily gobbled this down and equally happily noticed the large plastic bag of blueberry muffins on the counter.

"We have everything ready to go, Roger," Gail said as she and Mark cleared away the dishes. "Matthew should be here shortly to pick you up." Gail paused for a moment. "You can still change your mind, Roger. The veterinarian is right on our way out of the city."

"No thank you," Roger replied confidently. "It will be interesting—especially with blueberry muffins." Roger beamed a toothy dragon thanks at Gail.

Matthew showed up shortly afterward, and Roger bid Gail and Mark good-bye.

"Thanks for the muffins, Gail!" Roger called as he and Matthew left the house.

"Yes, thank you for the muffins," Matthew said. "See you in a week. Have fun, Mark!"

Roger looked around curiously upon entering Matthew's home. He noticed that the entrance contained many large plants, similar to the ones in Mark's greenhouse.

"You'll be staying in my room, Roger," said Matthew.

Roger noticed a slim, gray cat slide from beneath a sofa. The cat padded softly over to them.

"Hi, Ernie," Matthew said. "Roger, this is Ernie."

"Hi Ernie, I'm Roger."

"Hi, Roger," Ernie replied, glancing around.

Roger wondered why Ernie seemed so nervous, anxious even—when he heard Matthew give a soft cry.

"Uh oh," Matthew said.

Roger glanced down to see a pretty white cat with black and orange markings on her tail and one ear, staring up at him. Ernie had vanished as silently as he had appeared.

"Roger," said Matthew, "that is Sugar. I'll just set you up on this tree, and I'll put her downstairs. We'll go to my room afterward and have one of Gail's muffins."

"Okay," Roger replied while still returning the white cat's gaze. He flew up into a high branch of the tree. He was content to wait and look around. He was curious about Sugar, the white cat who sat rigidly on her hind legs and glared, emerald eyes on fire, at him.

Matthew bent down to pick Sugar up, but she avoided him and scurried away. Matthew chased after her ...

Matthew returned and said, "I guess we can get you to my room now. Fly down to my shoulder, and we'll go."

Roger flew down to Matthew's shoulder. They were just heading up to Matthew's room when a blur of white suddenly launched itself at Matthew's legs, almost knocking him over.

Roger flew up quickly and banged his scaly little head on the ceiling (much to his embarrassment). He recovered quickly and settled back down in the tree.

Maybe she is crazy, Roger thought to himself.

Matthew once again chased the white cat; Roger thought she seemed to be enjoying herself. He was certain he could hear her kitty laughter.

Well, she is leading him a merry chase, Roger thought.

Matthew returned shortly. He sounded a bit out of breath.

"I couldn't catch Sugar," he told Roger regretfully. "She is hiding somewhere. *Now* we can probably go to my room."

Roger was just about to fly down to Matthew's shoulder when he heard a phone ring in the background. (Roger knew what a phone was from Mark's house.)

"Oh, I better answer that," Matthew said. "I'll be right back."

Roger attempted to settle himself yet again in the tree when he realized his wings were tangled in the branches. As he tried to wriggle free, he lost his balance and flopped rather awkwardly to the floor. He looked up, and there was Sugar.

Sugar suddenly pounced, startling Roger so much that he didn't fly away. Fortunately, at the same moment, a blur of gray flew at Sugar, batting at her, and Roger felt himself being hauled away. He was in the hands of Ernie—the gray cat.

Ernie took Roger under the sofa.

"This is a good hiding spot," Ernie told Roger.

"Thank you, Ernie," Roger said. "She was so quick that I was too startled to fly away."

"I was watching," said Ernie. "I knew she would try something. She has always been playful, but lately she has been acting in an odd manner. It's not all the time; I can usually tell her mood by a certain look in her eyes."

Ernie glanced out from beneath the sofa. He checked for visible signs of Sugar. Then he sniffed and motioned for Roger to follow him out

"I don't see her. Let's get you back to the tree," Ernie said.

Roger flew, with Ernie trotting below, back into the tree. Ernie vanished beneath the sofa again after telling Roger that he would be looking out for him.

****

Sugar was sulking; Ernie had spoiled her fun with the strange, winged creature. A quick visit to her food dish made her feel much better, and she wandered back upstairs.

She noticed that the rather tall tree in the front entranceway looked different.

Sugar was familiar with the tree because she used it as part of one of her games. In this game, when the doorbell rang, Sugar would sit innocently under the leafy branches of the tree. She would sit there gazing at the unsuspecting visitor with her beautiful emerald eyes, purring loudly. Without fail, the visitor would be delighted and would reach out to pet Sugar; Sugar would then hiss and attack. This was one of Sugar's favorite games.

The tree seemed closed in; its limbs were gathered together like clouds on a stormy day. Sugar wandered closer and saw a pair of bright yellow-green eyes peering out at her—Roger.

"Come out of there," Sugar coaxed. "I'm not going to eat you."

****

Roger flew down cautiously and landed a couple of feet from Sugar. He was *not* going to let her surprise him again.

"I'm Sugar," announced the feline, self-importantly stretching her snowy limbs straight up. "And who and *what* are you?"

"I'm Roger, and I think I'm a dragon. I do know I'm not like anyone else I met on the ridge"

"And who did you meet on the ridge?" asked Sugar innocently.

Roger was losing his fear of Sugar and was wondering what all the fuss was about. After her pounce, she seemed quite pleasant.

He replied eagerly, "I met Tip, Soot, Jasper, Patch, and Jack." Roger described his friends to Sugar, who appeared to be listening very closely.

"Do they ever come around here?" asked Sugar.

"Yes, except for Jasper," Roger replied.

"I thought so," said Sugar thoughtfully. "I've seen birds and a squirrel in the tree beside our back porch, and a rabbit hopping around in our yard.

"Say, are you hungry?" Sugar asked suddenly.

Roger, although surprised by Sugar's abrupt change of topic, replied that he was in fact hungry.

"Wait here," Sugar said.

She scampered up the stairs. She returned quickly, dragging a loaf of bread.

"Quick, we've got to take this down to the pit and hide it. How fast are you?"

"I think I'm pretty fast," Roger stammered.

"Follow me but watch your head; the ceiling isn't as high down here," Sugar warned.

Roger flew carefully after Sugar. She ran down another flight of stairs and into a very low-ceilinged storage area. Roger followed her and saw that Ernie was there already.

"I thought I would tag along," Ernie said in response to Roger's questioning look.

Sugar ripped open the bread with her teeth and back claws. She fished out some bread for herself and Roger. Ernie did not want any bread.

"I don't like people food," Ernie told Roger.

Roger told them that he quite liked people food. Sugar and Ernie looked at him with surprise.

"Well, I like bread," Sugar said, "although my people really don't like it when I steal it off the counter."

"Why do you have to steal it?" asked Roger. "Don't your people give you enough to eat?" He was horrified at the thought of not having enough to eat. Ever since he had been found on the ridge, it seemed like everyone was always giving him food. He did not mind this at all.

"When Ernie and I were still kittens," Sugar replied, "we lived outside on our own. We never had enough to eat. Everyone like us snatched food from the others if we could, and we hid whatever we could find. Now that we are inside all of the time, this is not a problem, but I guess old habits die hard."

"Why are you inside all of the time?" Roger asked.

"We don't have claws, and our people agreed to keep us in when they adopted us," replied Sugar.

"Oh," said Roger weakly. He was kind of at a loss for words. Even in his brief time on this earth, he could not imagine what it would be like to be inside all of the time.

"We're okay with it," Ernie said. "We're quite comfortable inside. Soft cushions to sleep on, lots of food to eat."

"You can speak for yourself," Sugar retorted. She looked sad.

"Do you want to go outside?" asked Roger. He was starting to feel sorry for Sugar.

"Every time you sneak outside," Ernie interrupted, before Sugar could reply, "you are terrified."

"That's not the point." Sugar sniffed. She did not say what the point *was*, however.

"You go outside, Roger, right?" Sugar asked.

"Yes," Roger replied. He felt even worse for the pretty, odd white cat. "I have claws, however, and wings."

*****

Sugar watched carefully as Roger munched on his bread. She was jealous of the little dragon. She knew that she couldn't be outside anymore, but even with the all of time that had passed, she could still remember the fragrant smells. She remembered gentle breezes and chasing butterflies.

Sugar had asked Roger about his ridge friends on purpose. His feathered friends and the squirrel sometimes sat in the crabapple tree outside the patio doors. She knew that they knew she could not go outside, and they seemed to delight in teasing her about it.

What Sugar was actually planning was a little payback to her furry, feathered tormentors. She suspected they would wonder about Roger and would show up in the tree looking for him. Once they arrived, there she would be, at the patio doors, with Roger at her side. It would drive them bonkers. Roger would make an amusing toy too. Imagine a flying thing to chase! It would be like chasing a butterfly again.

****

Roger, although a very smart, sensitive little dragon, could not read minds. He was blissfully unaware of Sugar's plot.

Sugar is not so bad, he thought.

"What do we do now?" asked Roger. His bread was gone, and he was very curious about his new surroundings. He secretly wished he could go outside; his friends might be there.

"Well, I'm going to take a nap," Sugar replied. "Can you fly back upstairs?"

Roger followed Sugar and Ernie to a cozy-looking family room. The cats jumped onto a sofa and settled down for their nap. Roger flopped down next to them.

At that moment, Matthew appeared and joined the animals on the sofa. He petted Sugar and Ernie and picked Roger up.

"Are you okay, Roger?" Matthew asked. "I'm sorry. I didn't mean to be so long. I've set up a bed for you in my room, and I always keep my door closed." Matthew gave the cats a pointed glance.

"We've been fine," Roger said. He decided not to mention Sugar's pounce or the stolen bread.

"Can he understand you?" asked Ernie.

"Yes," Roger replied.

"I don't think he understands *exactly* what we're saying," Ernie continued thoughtfully, "but he seems to get the general idea."

"We can understand humans perfectly," Sugar said lazily, and resumed her nap.

A delicious, familiar aroma wafted up the stairs. Roger recognized it as pizza!

He was still hungry; the bread had helped some, but it had not filled his tummy.

He looked around and saw a tall, big human coming up the stairs. The word *Viking* popped into Roger's head. The Viking was carrying two large pizza boxes.

"Is that a dragon? How is that possible?" he asked, looking at Roger.

"Yes, I believe he *is* a dragon," Matthew replied. "I looked up pictures on the Internet, and he looks like a miniature dragon—I'll show you later, Roger—I don't think he breathes fire, however."

Who would want to breathe fire? Roger thought to himself.

"We found him on the ridge," Matthew said quickly, before Roger had a chance to speak up. "Or, rather, Sheila did. His name is Roger. He can talk and understands us and everything." Matthew launched into the details of how Roger had been found and where he had been staying.

"Roger is staying with us until Gail and Mark get back from their trip," Matthew said in conclusion.

"You found him on the ridge?" the Viking asked, puzzled. "Well, that is curious." He put the pizza boxes on the coffee table. He reached down and gently picked Roger up. Roger instantly sensed that this huge Viking was kind. His green-gold eyes stared up at him fearlessly.

"I'm Christopher," the tall boy said. "I am Matthew's brother."

"Hi, Christopher," said Roger happily.

Christopher set Roger back down with the cats, who had been watching the exchange.

"Where is he going to sleep?" Christopher asked Matthew, throwing Sugar a glance.

"He'll stay in my room; he'll be no problem. He eats whatever we do, and he especially likes pizza."

Chris grabbed the pizza boxes off the coffee table. Roger eyed them longingly.

"Well, let's get a couple of plates then," he said to Matthew, and they headed to the kitchen.

****

Sugar jumped off the sofa and stalked to the patio doors, the mirror for her tormentors. There sat Jack, Soot, Patch, and Tip. The birds and Patch were hanging out in the crabapple tree, right outside the doors. Tip was at the base of the tree.

The game is on, thought Sugar. She quickly ran back into the family room.

"Roger," she sang, "your friends are outside." Roger flew after Sugar to the patio doors.

Sugar saw the outside critters react when they saw Roger beside her. Jack and Soot started tapping at the glass with their beaks; Patch was running back and forth across the railing; Tip was hopping around the tree. Sugar smiled to herself and swatted Roger with a paw. The reaction was everything Sugar had wished for and more. There was squealing, more pecking, and anxious chatter. Their voices chorused like a band warming up.

"How could we have let him come here?"

"We could have looked after him."

Sugar, delighted that her plan had worked, was just about to give Roger another slap when she saw Matthew and Chris coming out of the kitchen.

"Sugar, leave Roger alone!" Matthew cried angrily.

Sugar took off, leaving Roger in her wake. She had achieved her desired effect—a wee bit of payback against her tormentors. Sugar was now happy to hide somewhere until her boys were a little less miffed with her.

Now, to be told, Sugar did not understand why she acted out at times.

I'm actually a nice, friendly cat, most of the time, she thought as she fled downstairs.

She suspected that her attack mode had a great deal to do with being abandoned as a kitten and having to fend for herself in the wild. She wondered why she didn't just hide like Ernie.

Well, I'm hiding now, she said to herself as she slipped into the crawlspace.

Sugar knew her attack episodes were becoming more frequent. In fact, she found herself locked up in the downstairs family room on occasion. She knew deep inside that something was wrong with her, but she just didn't understand what it could be.

Sugar, hiding, was now feeling bad for swatting Roger.

I'll tell him that I'm sorry later, she said to herself.

****

Upstairs, a confused Roger was back on the sofa with Ernie.

Matthew had told Roger that he felt very badly about leaving him alone with Sugar.

"I was not worried. She seemed friendly, and then whoosh," Roger replied.

"I know; we can never tell when she's going to misbehave," Matthew said. "That is why we should not have left you alone with her. She did seem fine, however."

"Your friends are still outside. Do you want to pop out and say hello and let them know you're okay? After that, we can have pizza."

"Yes, I would like to do that," Roger replied. He glanced toward the patio doors. "Although it looks like they've settled down."

Once outside, Roger's friends quickly surrounded him.

"That dreadful Sugar," Patch squeaked.

"Are you hurt?" asked Soot anxiously.

"Do you want to fly away with us?" Jack and Soot asked together.

"I have to say you were right about her rather odd behavior," Roger replied carefully. "She attacked me as soon as I got here. Ernie took me to a hiding spot and then put me in a tree for safekeeping. After that, however, she was nice, and then *not* so nice. She has no claws, so she did not hurt me."

"Do you want to come away with us? We can keep you safe until you can go back to Mark's house," said Jack.

"No thank you. I will be okay. Matthew and said they would keep a better eye. I will be more cautious as well. I'll just fly out of her reach if she starts getting scary. I noticed that her eyes kind of glitter just before she does something scary."

After that rambling speech, Roger realized that he was quite hungry and there was pizza waiting. He said good-bye to his friends, then flew back onto the porch, where Matthew was waiting to let him back inside.

The three boys ate pizza. Ernie joined them, not for pizza but to settle on the sofa, purring away.

"I'm glad you are okay, Roger," Ernie told him. "I had no idea Sugar was going to do that. I would have stopped her."

"She didn't hurt me," Roger said. "I don't think that she even wanted to hurt me. Where is she now?"

"She is probably hiding in the crawlspace. There was still bread left, so she may hide there for a while," Ernie replied.

The eve of Roger's initial meeting with crazy white cat ended peacefully.

Roger settled in Matthew's room, and he watched Matthew play computer games for a while.

"Roger," Matthew said suddenly, "I said I would show you some pictures of a dragon that I found. I've brought them up on my computer screen again, if you are interested."

Roger was very interested. He flew from his comfy bed in Matthew's closet and landed on Matthew's shoulder. On the screen, Roger saw a picture of a critter that looked a great deal like him. Roger had caught glances of himself in the mirrors hanging in Mark and Matthew's homes; he most definitely did not look like any of his friends.

"See?" Matthew declared happily. "You're a mini dragon!"

"I hope I don't get *that* big," Roger stated, pointing to the screen. He secretly did not think that he would get much bigger. It was just a feeling he had.

"I *am* a kind of dragon," Roger said to himself as he settled back into his nest. Roger found this confirmation of what he had guessed to be comforting. He soon fell into a deep sleep.

Chapter 12

Another Visit with Kobe and Bear

The next morning, Matthew and Roger had dry Fruit Loops in the kitchen. Roger enjoyed the Fruit Loops. They weren't Gail's muffins, nor were they her pancakes, but they were tasty. Ernie was snoozing on the sofa, and Sugar had not yet reappeared. Roger was relieved about this.

After breakfast, Matthew let Roger into the backyard. He provided a paper bag with a couple of apples, some popcorn, and a large plastic water bottle. These he put in the shade under the porch.

"See you in a couple of hours, Roger," Matthew said. "We'll have lunch. I'll just be playing on the computer in my room, if you need me. You can just tap on the patio door, and I'll hear you. I might look for Sugar first. I don't like it when she hides for a long time."

"I'll be fine outside," Roger told him. "I'll visit with my friends."

Soot, Jack, Tip, and Patch were all waiting for Roger.

"Jasper said to say hello," said Jack. "Did you want to fly to the ridge today?"

"I wanted to stay by the birdfeeder," Patch whined. "I don't feel like tree hopping today."

"I'd like try to find Kobe and Bear again," Roger replied hopefully. "Tip, you and Patch wouldn't be able to come, as it's not very close for anyone without wings."

Or a bus, he thought, recalling his foolhardy excursion.

"We'll fly with you," Soot said. "Won't we, Jack?" Jack readily agreed.

"Hopefully, you remember where it is," Jack teased. "You *did* get there most of the way by a *bus*."

"I think so," Roger said. "We can give it a try."

It was decided that the scaly and feathered winged ones would try to find Kobe and Bear. They would then meet up with the others on the ridge.

"Well, that gives me lots of time at the birdfeeder," Patch said happily.

****

Sugar had come out of hiding as the friends were discussing their plans for the day. She stared out of the french doors at them. She, for once, did not fly into a rage at seeing her tormentors; she saw Roger as well.

I wish I could join him, she thought.

To her surprise, there was suddenly a flurry of wings, a scampering of paws, and the entire group vanished, including Roger.

"I've scared him away!" she meowed aloud, in her alarm.

Ernie appeared at her side.

"Scared who away?" he asked.

"Roger!" Sugar answered him, upset. "He flew away with his feathered friends."

"Matthew must have let him outside," Ernie said. "He did say that he could go outside."

"I just know he flew away, and it's probably my fault," cried Sugar.

"Well, you were bullying him yesterday," scolded Ernie.

"It was just a little fun."

"Including the pounce when he first arrived?"

Sugar had no reply for that. As mentioned, she didn't know why she flew into rages.

"He was with his friends?" Ernie asked. Sugar nodded. "He'll be in safe wings then, and I'm sure they'll bring him home. Plus, I saw the way he was gobbling pizza yesterday." Ernie shuddered a bit at this. "How anyone could prefer pizza to Miss Meow salmon is beyond me. The point is he'll get hungry."

Sugar agreed that there was nothing much that they could do. Both cats jumped on the sofa and settled down for a snooze. Sugar hoped that Roger would come home soon.

****

Roger and his feathered companions were in the community of Edgemont. As they approached the Nose Hill natural park, Roger started looking down. His acute vision finally settled on a familiar-looking yard and the two large brown and black dogs sitting within.

"There they are!" he cried triumphantly and swirled down to land in the branches of the same tree he had landed in before. Jack and Soot landed on the same branch as Roger, which caused the tree to shake a bit. They were large birds, and Roger, although he was a miniature dragon, was still a good size.

Both dogs noticed the shaking tree. Bear immediately rushed over, barking. Kobe struggled to his legs and hobbled after Bear. Roger peered down into Bear's chocolate-brown eyes.

"Hi, Bear, Kobe," Roger said to his two doggy friends.

"Roger!" they replied in surprise. "What are you doing here?"

Roger flew to the ground.

"What are you doing?" cried Soot.

"I told you about Kobe and Bear," Roger reminded his friend. "They are friendly."

"They're just so big," Soot muttered.

To the dogs, Roger said, "I wanted to see how you were doing." Roger was more concerned about how Kobe was doing but decided it would be more polite to include both dogs.

Kobe had collapsed back down on the ground, and Bear sat back on his hind legs.

"We're doing very well," Bear replied.

"You can speak for yourself," Kobe interrupted.

"How are *you*, Roger?" Bear continued. "I take it you arrived home safely?"

Roger told them about seeing his boys as he was flying toward the mountains.

"I was very happy to see them," Roger said, "but I probably would never have found them if you hadn't helped, Bear."

"Aw, it was nothing, kid. We couldn't have you flying all over the neighborhood. You're not exactly ordinary looking."

"Bear, that wasn't polite!" Kobe cried.

"Sorry, Roger," Bear muttered, rolling his eyes. "But you *aren't* ordinary looking."

Roger was aware that he looked like none of his furry or feathered friends and had not taken offense. However, he did not know what Bear meant by "ordinary." All of his friends looked different from each other. He decided to get down to the true reason for his visit.

"How are your legs, Kobe? How is your back?" Roger asked.

"I'm better at certain times." Kobe struggled again to his feet, ambled a few steps, ambled back, and flopped back down. "Other times, well, I'm not so good."

"What have *you* been up to?" Kobe asked Roger.

Roger told them about Jasper's narrow escape and his recent move to Matthew's house.

"They have two cats," he added. "Ernie is shy but nice. Sugar can be nice, but ..." His voice trailed off. He told them about her attacking him upon his arrival and her actions at the french doors.

"We don't like cats on principle," said Kobe. "But that Sugar sounds strange, even for a cat."

"Maybe there's something wrong with her," said Bear.

Roger thought about that. He had only just met Sugar, but maybe there *was* something wrong with her. His friends had told him stories about hearing her shriek like a cougar and about her occasionally stopping her people from entering their own house.

There was rustling above. Roger looked up to see the two birds sitting there. They had come out of hiding.

"Roger," called Jack, "shouldn't we be going?"

"Who are they?" asked Bear. Kobe and Bear stared at the two curiously.

"My friends. They were part of the group that found me on the ridge. We should be heading home." Roger flew back up into the tree.

"I'm getting kind of hungry and sleepy anyway," Bear said.

"I am too," Kobe added.

"If you can, come back and visit again," the dogs chorused.

The dog run was nearby. Kobe carefully picked his way over to it, followed closely by Bear.

Roger, Jack, and Soot flew to the ridge.

"Why were you so anxious to see Kobe and Bear?" asked Soot. "Not that they didn't seem nice," he added hastily.

"I wanted to check up on Kobe. It's a long story," Roger hedged. "Remember I told you how sad he looked when I first met him?"

Roger was glad they had gone to see Bear and Kobe. He resolved to speak with Mel very soon.

Chapter 13

Talking with Eagles

Roger and his buddies flew back to Matthew's yard, before going to the ridge. (Roger had forgotten that Matthew had said he would come out in a couple of hours, and they would have lunch.) Roger quickly gobbled some snacks, and the birds raided the feeder. After they were all full, they flew off to the ridge to meet the others.

They found Jasper, Tip, and Patch in a thicket about two thirds of the way down the hill leading to the still swollen river. The three had been watching and emerged when the threesome landed. Roger and Jasper shared happy greetings, as they had not seen each other since Jasper's rescue. Patch and Tip had filled Jasper in about Roger's move to the "House of Sugar."

"How was it in there with her?" Jasper asked. "I heard about the pouncing and the little show Sugar staged for the benefit of the guys outside. I'm glad to see you are none the worse for wear."

"I quite like Matthew, and his brother Chris is very nice as well. Ernie is very friendly," Roger replied. "I thought it sad that he and Sugar cannot go outside, but they have no claws, and Sugar could take it into her head to attack someone much bigger than she is."

"I'd place money on Sugar," Jasper muttered. "The guys have told me about her piercing shrieks."

Roger told them that Bear thought there might be something wrong with Sugar.

"Yeah, she's *crazy*," Jasper said.

Jasper told Roger that he had not been down to the river to fish since being rescued. "I thought I was a goner for sure. I have never seen the river rise so quickly, and I've been around for a while." Jasper shuddered at the memory. "I saw pieces of humans' homes float away."

"I think it was all of this wood from those homes along the riverbank that saved you," Jack said thoughtfully. "It kept your log from being swept away."

"I'm staying away from the river for a while," Jasper said. "Getting back to Sugar," he said to Roger, "I'd just keep out of her way, if possible."

"I'll just fly away from her. She has taken me by surprise a couple of times. I will be a great deal more cautious now.

"I'd like to fly up to see Mel and Milly. I need to ask Mel something," Roger then said.

"Do you want us to come with you?" asked his feathered friends.

"No thank you; it's personal. I won't be long." At this, Roger launched himself into the air and flew up to the nest.

I hope Mel is around, he thought to himself.

Upon his arrival, there was no Mel but only a frazzled-looking Milly (if eagles can look frazzled, that is) with her two eaglets.

"Oh, hi, Roger," Milly said. "Max! Quit standing on the end of the nest! Your dad and I have told you to give it a few more days. You're not strong enough yet!

"Sorry, Roger," Milly said. "These little scamps are anxious to fly, but they're not quite ready." Max had climbed down from his perch and was now making a show of ignoring his mother and grooming himself.

"Er, is Mel around?" Roger asked.

"Oh." Milly sounded a little hurt, but she replied evenly, "No, he's gone fishing further downstream, where the river is not as rough. Is there something that I can do for you?"

Roger thought for a moment and then spoke in a low voice. "Do you know about the meadow?"

"Oh yes!" Milly replied eagerly. "All of the forest creatures know about the meadow. How do you know about it?"

"Well, Mel showed it me," Roger replied.

"You're very lucky. Usually it doesn't appear until one of us is ready to go there."

"How does one get there?"

"We eagles fly there, because to us it appears high up. I imagine it appears down below for the four-legged creatures. Why do you have all of this interest in the meadow?"

"I have a friend." Roger told Milly about Kobe. "Would Kobe be able to go there?"

"All living creatures go there eventually."

"But he can't walk very well," Roger stammered.

"As soon as he's ready, the meadow will appear before him, and all of his troubles will vanish. He will be like a young puppy again. The meadow restores youth and energy."

At this moment, Mel swooped into the nest, carrying a large salmon in his beak. "Lunchtime!" he called. (Max finally perked up at that.)

"Well, hello, Roger! It is good to see you! Would you like some fish?" Mel was busily tearing off strips of salmon and offering these to Max and Billy.

"No thank you," Roger declined hastily.

"Good to see you," Mel repeated after the salmon had been gobbled up by the eaglets and their parents. "What brings you here?" he asked.

"Oh," Milly interrupted hastily, "he's here to ask about the meadow and a friend of his who is unwell. He told me he saw it, but he was with you, wasn't he? You're rather good at seeing it when others cannot."

"Well, I'm delighted that you thought of the meadow," Mel said thoughtfully. "What was your question?" Roger explained again his concerns about Kobe.

"Worthy concerns," said Mel. "Much is unknown about the meadow. We eagles have long been honored by many humans as rulers of the sky, possessed with grace, power, intellect, and ancient knowledge. I believe it is this knowledge that gives us a deeper sense of the meadow. Not many other creatures, human or not, have this gift. It is sad in a way, but in another, when they do discover the meadow in all its splendor, it will be such an enormous gift." Mel paused for a moment, he then continued.

"I believe each living creature finds what they are seeking in the meadow,"

"Dad, you talk too much," this was whined by, guess who? You got it, Max

Mel shook his regal head and bowed apologetically to Roger. "Max is quite correct. I do tend to go on and on."

****

Far below, Roger's other friends were beginning to be concerned. Where is he? they wondered. Did the eagles eat him? Did the eaglets eat him? This was quite silly of them to think, as the eagles had rescued Jasper. Old ideas crept in—their past fears of the eagles—and they all stared upward in terror. No one was actually brave enough to go up and check. Now, Patch and Jasper could be excused, as they could not fly. For the others, however, there was no excuse. This was especially true of Jack, as he knew exactly where the nest was.

****

The noise from below eventually floated up to the nest, like a wisp of poplar tree cotton. Roger paid immediate attention.

"Oh, I should go!" said Roger. "I told them I would not be long!"

"Yes, you are right, Roger," Mel agreed. "I forgot how protective your friends are of you—and that is how it should be. We eagles are still a puzzle for many. Your friends probably are very concerned. Although you would think they would feel differently after meeting me."

Mel bowed his head once again and added, "We forest creatures are born with the knowledge of the meadow. Your friend Kobe may not have this knowledge. It might ease him, in his own mind, to realize that the meadow is always there and that he will be able to run and jump again."

Roger was much relieved by his conversation with the eagles. He resolved to contact Kobe and Bear as soon as possible and share this conversation with them. In the meantime, however, he took his leave of the eagles and flew back down to his frantic friends.

"We were just getting ready to fly up and check on you," said Soot.

"I'm fine," Roger replied thoughtfully. He was wondering how soon he could fly back and visit with Kobe and Bear. He was also wondering about Sugar.

"I'd better fly home," Roger added.

Roger, Soot, and Jack flew back to Matthew's yard. Roger visited with his friends until the screen door opened, and Matthew appeared.

"I lost track of time," Matthew told Roger. "Let's have some lunch!"

Roger bid his friends good-bye and happily followed Matthew into the house. He had been getting quite hungry.

"We're glad you are back," the cats sang as Roger flew inside.

"Roger, I've been feeling very guilty about the way I behaved earlier," Sugar began. "I want to apologize."

Roger flew to the top of a plant holder—*I'm simply being careful*, he thought—and waited for Sugar to continue.

"I don't know why I behave in such a manner," she confessed. "I just get this funny feeling inside. While living outside, I had to fight many times, small as I was, just to survive. I live here now, though, and have been here for some time, and I am safe. I guess it is like stealing the bread; it doesn't make sense to steal and hide food when I've plenty, and it doesn't make sense to attack when I'm safe."

"I guess I am cowardly," said Ernie. "I always hid if I felt threatened. I still do. It's kind of embarrassing actually."

****

Roger shared—yes, you guessed it—another pizza with Matthew and Christopher and thought about his discussion with Kobe and Bear. Maybe there was something wrong with Sugar. He wondered how serious it was and if the meadow was close to her, but she did not know. This was food for thought, just as the pizza had been food for his rumbling tummy.

Chapter 14

A Lost Eaglet

Jasper was restless; he did not fish a great deal, as a rule, and being stranded in the river had thrown him off, but he was longing for fresh fish. Looking down at the river from his snug hiding place, he could tell that the river's wrath was subsiding.

"I'm going to wander down again," he told himself. Driven by hunger and an appetite for something other than leaves and berries, Jasper trotted down the cliffs (he remained hidden, naturally).

Jasper peered out of his leafy shelter to ensure that there was no one about—of the two-legged critter variety, that is—and ran to the shore of the river. Once there, he was surprised to hear the cries of eagles overhead; this was not a usual occurrence.

The eagles were normally very shy and very private. Jasper glanced up just as Mel landed at his feet. Now, even though Jasper had met Mel before, he still struck a very imposing presence.

"Mel," Jasper said, "is something wrong?"

"Jasper, we've lost Max, our oldest eaglet. He has been intent on trying his wings for some time, and he is not quite ready. Today, he flung himself off the nest while we were not looking.

"We can see from high above, but the woods are so thick. We are not suited to scrambling through the woods, with our wingspan and claws. Might you look for him, please, down here? He might have fallen."

Jasper readily agreed. He had been wondering for some time about how to repay his feathered saviors but had not been able to think of anything. This sounded like just the thing, and he sincerely hoped he would find Max and find him safe.

After Mel flew away, Jasper hurriedly rounded up Tip, Patch, Jack, and Soot and told them about Max.

"Will you two please go and fetch Roger?" Jasper asked Jack and Soot. The two birds flew off right away.

****

Roger was out in Matthew's backyard, munching on an apple. He looked up happily as Jack and Soot landed on the branch above his head.

"Hi," Roger called to the birds.

Jack got right to the issue at hand. "Roger, Max is lost. Jasper told Mel that we would help look for him."

Roger was alarmed upon hearing this story; he wasted no time.

"Let's go," he said. The three friends, feathered and scaly, flew quickly back to the clearing where Jasper, Tip, and Patch were waiting.

"Good to see you, Roger," the three voiced as one when Roger arrived.

"Thanks for letting me know," Roger replied.

"I thought Soot, Patch, and I could look close to the ground," said Jasper. "And, Roger, you and the birds can search in higher branches." Roger agreed, and everyone went off in different directions.

Roger flew into a grove of trees. The tree that was crowned by the eagle's nest was within this grove. He circled through the branches, being careful not to get his wings stuck, higher and higher.

"Max, it's me, Roger," he called.

A rustling above his head startled Roger. He flew up carefully and found Max huddled within the branches.

"Max!" Roger cried joyfully. "Are you okay?"

"Hi, Roger," Max replied. "I'm fine. I flew all the way down here. Well, I *may* have fallen part of the way. I was doing great until my wings got tired."

Jack and Soot circled a few feet away.

"I found Max," Roger called. The birds flew over.

"Would you please stay with him, Jack, while I fly up to the nest?" Roger asked. After Jack settled on the branches above Max, Roger flew up to the nest. There he found a very worried Milly.

"We found Max!" announced Roger. "And he is fine. Jack is with him."

"Oh that is wonderful! Thank you!" Milly gasped in relief.

"Jasper rounded everyone up and organized the search party," Roger told her. He wanted to give credit where credit was due.

"I must thank Jasper and go find Mel," Milly said. "Then we can help Max back to the nest. Roger, would you please stay with Billy until I return?"

Roger agreed, of course, and Milly took off after warning Billy not to pull his brother's trick.

"Roger, make sure he doesn't try to climb to the top of the nest," Milly added. Roger privately hoped that Billy would not decide to climb to the top of the nest. He did not think he would be able to stop him.

"Max scared me. I'm staying right here," Billy said, as if reading Roger's mind.

****

Milly found the others in Jasper's favorite clearing in the forest. The others did not run off when she landed but did move a respectable distance away. Milly thanked them all individually.

"If you hadn't brought everyone together, I don't know when we would have found Max," Milly said, turning to Jasper. "I'm going find Mel. But first, would one of you please take me to where Max is?"

"I'll show you," Soot said.

Milly followed Soot to where Max was perched, well back in the foliage, blending in quite well. Jack was a vivid blue against the branches.

"Hi, Mum!" Max chirped boldly.

"Am I relieved to see you," Milly replied. "I'm just going to find your father, and we'll fly with you back to the nest. I believe I see him now." Milly was glancing upward with her keen gaze. "I'll go grab him and be right back."

Max and Milly returned quickly. Max and the birds watched their approach.

"Max, can you manage to get onto my back?" asked Mel.

Max obediently climbed, somewhat awkwardly, onto his father's back.

"Cling tightly with your claws and, if possible, beak to my back and neck," advised Mel. When Max was secure, Mel took off for the nest. Milly flew beneath, keeping an eagle eye on the two forms.

Finally, they made it back to the nest. Mel flew in, and Max tumbled off his father's back.

****

Roger had been waiting anxiously for the eagles to return. He was much relieved when the three appeared, followed closely by Jack, and Max was back in the nest.

"I don't want to have to do that again," Mel told Roger, ruffling the feathers on his back carefully. "Max has very sharp claws and beak."

"Most importantly," he added, eying his two sons sternly, "I do not want to have occasion to do that again. You frightened us very much, Max, and you could have been badly hurt."

"Thank you, Roger, for staying in the nest, and we are both forever grateful for the two of you and all the others who took part in the search." Mel finished this speech with a bow of his proud head.

"Now, I should go fishing; these two have not had anything to eat. Please tell the others that the next time I see them, I'll thank them personally." Mel gave another bow of his head and flew off to fetch lunch. Milly said thank you again, and Roger, with Jack, flew back to the clearing.

Roger was glad to see that the others were still waiting. He told the group that Max was safe and repeated the eagles' thanks.

"And, I want to thank you as well," Roger added. "The eagles are my friends, too. Jasper, I especially want to thank *you* for organizing the search. Now, I better fly home; Matthew may be looking for me."

Roger glanced down as he flew home and smiled as he saw his friends melt into the woods.

They are probably as hungry as I am, he thought.

Chapter 15

Roger Remains with Sugar and Ernie

Roger, Sugar, and Ernie were curled up on the sofa watching television one rainy summer afternoon; that is, Roger was watching the television—Sugar and Ernie were snoozing. Roger was quite handy with the remote. He enjoyed watching the moving, speaking figures darting across the screen. When he first saw television, Roger had been a bit puzzled; these moving figures looked real, unlike the characters in one of the boys' games.

"They are like reflections in a river," Mark had explained, "a picture of the reality."

To be honest, Roger had not really understood this, but he still enjoyed playing with the "remote," as the boys called it, when he was alone with Sugar and Ernie and not outside with his other buddies.

Roger was thinking as he fiddled with the remote. He thought that he had settled nicely into Matthew's household. He enjoyed his furry inside friends. Sugar had not played any more tricks on him, and Ernie—well, Ernie was just a gentle critter.

"I do sense sadness in Sugar," Roger said to himself as he flipped to a different channel. "She almost reminds me of when I first met Kobe. I wonder if her sadness is somehow due to her moods. I would like to help her if I can." Roger glanced at his sleeping friends. He thought that helping Sugar would also help Ernie. Sugar and Ernie were best buds, *except* when Sugar flew into one of her rages. Roger had noted that Ernie fought back now, and that usually settled Sugar's mood.

****

Sugar was also deep in thought as she catnapped in front of the television. She realized that she very much liked her winged friend. Roger was friendly and talkative, and when she was in one of her rages, he just flew away. Ernie had taken to fighting back, which frankly surprised her. She used to be able to scare him. Sugar was content right now, catnapping on the sofa, but she never knew when that feeling would overtake her usual sunny disposition.

Sugar, forever inside, had adopted Roger in her mind. Sugar scolded herself whenever she remembered (she was losing track of when she lost her temper) tormenting Roger. She realized that Ernie was glad to have someone else to talk to; she grew so moody at times. She hated acting out. She was her usual, fat, furry purring self when suddenly a cougar would emerge.

****

Roger, lost in his thoughts, almost did not notice that Matthew was standing in front of the sofa.

"Hey, Roger, Mark is home. You can go back over there if you would like to."

Sugar and Ernie looked at Roger with alarmed expressions on their furry faces.

"Ask if you can stay," Sugar whispered to him.

"We don't want you to go back," Ernie added.

Roger made up his mind very quickly. Roger sensed that both cats needed his company, especially Sugar, and he was reluctant to leave them.

"Can't I stay here?" he asked in a shaking voice. He opened his already big eyes as wide as he could and gazed pleadingly at Matthew. (Roger knew how to play his cards—those big eyes, shaking voice. He *was* magical, after all.)

"Of course you can," Matthew stammered. "It's been great having you here. I just better text Mark and let him know."

Roger knew that Mark and Matthew talked to each other with a small handheld computer. Matthew told him that it was called a cell phone. He watched as Matthew removed this gadget from his pocket and started tapping away.

"Mark is curious as to *why* you want to stay with Sugar and Ernie," Matthew said suddenly, looking up from his phone.

"I've become quite attached to the two of them," Roger replied slowly. "I really like Sheila, too. She goes outside, however, and I can visit her there. Sugar and Ernie do not go outside. It would be difficult to visit them if I moved back to Mark's."

"Sugar *does* seem to be behaving better," Matthew said thoughtfully. He started tapping away at the phone again.

"All set," Matthew said after a few minutes. "They are disappointed, Roger, but want you to know that if you change your mind, you can go there anytime. Right now, we're invited to supper."

Roger greeted this news happily; he was very hungry. He was also a wee bit flattered; Sugar and Ernie wanted him to stay with them, and Mark wanted him over there. *I'm quite the popular little dragon,* he thought. He was glad that he could stay with Sugar; he had not had a chance to talk with her about ... things.

Roger was greeted with much enthusiasm when he and Matthew arrived at Mark's house for supper. Gail had made pizza, much to Roger's delight. After the pizza was eaten and very much enjoyed, Roger followed Sheila outside.

"It is good to see you, Roger," said Sheila. "How have you been? How was it with Sugar?"

"I've been very well, thank you," Roger replied. "Sugar acted strangely when I first arrived. She apologized, and we have gotten along fine ever since. She still behaves oddly at times, but I just fly out of her way. Did you have fun at the veterinarian's house?"

"I had lots of fun. They have three dogs, so I had many playmates. I am glad to be home, however. Speaking of home, I overheard Mark telling Gail that you have decided to stay at Matthew's?" Sheila gave Roger a puzzled look.

"Yes. I can always fly over here and visit you and go inside with you to see Mark and Gail. Sugar and Ernie do not go outside. If I was living here, I'd probably never see them except through the glass."

At that moment, Matthew appeared at the patio doors and called to Roger that they should be going home.

"I'll pop by tomorrow," Roger assured Sheila. He flew inside, thanked Gail again for the delicious pizza, said good night, and followed Matthew home.

Chapter 16
Roger Meets a New Friend

T he next few days flew by. Roger was outside most of the day, visiting with Sheila and his ridge friends. He did not see Matthew except at supper, but he knew that Matthew hung around with *his* friends and did not mind.

One day, Roger came in for supper to find Matthew sitting in the family room. He was staring at his phone and looking somewhat strange. *How odd,* Roger thought. *He usually goes to his room to be on his computer.*

"Oh, hi, Roger," Matthew said absently as Roger settled himself on the sofa next to him.

"Is something wrong?" asked Roger.

"Er no, nothing is wrong. My aunt May is coming home. She sent me a text." Matthew waved his phone at Roger, as if to highlight his comment, and went on to explain: "Aunt May lives with us when she is not travelling. I have not seen her for a while."

"That should be good news," Roger risked saying.

"It is. It's just—oh boy, this is awkward—I'm not sure what her reaction to you will be."

"Oh." Roger was thoughtful. "I guess we'll have to wait and see. When does she arrive?"

"She'll be here in a couple of days. I guess there is no point worrying about it. Let's eat! We're having tacos."

Tacos were another favorite of Roger's. He happily accepted his plate, and he and Matthew ate together contentedly.

On the afternoon that Aunt May was due to arrive, Matthew asked Roger to remain in his room until he came in to get him. It was a beautiful Saturday, and Roger would much rather have been outside, but he agreed.

"May I have a snack, please?" he asked politely. Matthew grabbed him a mini bag of salt and vinegar potato chips, which Roger loved, and Roger settled happily on his box to munch, crunch, and wait.

It was a short while later when Roger heard an unfamiliar voice. *That must be Aunt May*, he thought. Sugar had shown him how to open regular doors—a combination of batting at the doorknob and pulling with her paws at the bottom. Roger was able to grasp the doorknob with his little dragon hand, and he did so now. Curiously, Roger peered out from around the door.

A tall, sturdy lady stood at the entrance to the family room with suitcases at her feet. Matthew and Christopher were standing next to her. Roger was surprised to see Christopher; when home, he rarely came out of what Matthew called his "man cave," except to prepare meals.

"How are you boys?" she asked, giving them both big hugs. "How did everything go while I was gone?" She beamed at the boys. Her broad, freckled face was tan and smiling.

"I have some goodies for both of you in these bags somewhere," she continued. "Why don't I just unpack, get settled, and then we'll have a good visit." Each boy grabbed a suitcase and headed in Roger's direction. He quickly darted back inside Matthew's room and pushed the door closed.

Roger heard the door of the room next to Matthew's open, followed by the sounds of drawers opening and closing. The spare room door closed again, and Roger heard footsteps heading past Matthew's door toward the family room. Roger pulled the door open from the bottom— he had not closed it tightly—and looked out again. He did not see anyone.

They must be sitting on the sofa, he thought. He could hear the low murmur of voices but could not quite make out the words.

Roger was *so* curious. There was a new person to meet, and an adult one at that. Roger's experience with grown-up critters of the human variety had been limited to Gail. He did not count Christopher; Roger felt that Christopher was still holding on to his childhood in many ways.

If only I could get closer, whined his snoopy internal voice.

I was told to wait, Roger reminded himself.

The nosy dragon finally won the argument, and Roger slipped quietly out of Matthew's room. He flattened himself against the wall and crept toward the family room. He stopped as soon as he could hear everything that was being said yet remain out of sight.

"Thank you for all of the gifts, Aunt May," Matthew was saying.

"Yes, thank you," echoed Christopher.

"You are very welcome!" Aunt May chirped.

"Aunt May," Matthew said suddenly. "There is something I should tell you."

"Hmmm," Aunt May replied. "You do seem a bit restless. What's going on?"

Matthew finally said, "Mark and I were on the ridge, trying to catch Sheila, and we found something."

"Ooh!" exclaimed Aunt May excitedly. "What did you find? A dinosaur bone? I've never heard of any dinosaur bones being found on the ridge, but stranger things have happened. And that shouldn't make you uncomfortable, unless you were planning on keeping it and not turning it over to a museum?"

"No, he's not a fossil."

"Did you say *he*?" quizzed Aunt May.

"His name is Roger, and I think he's some kind of dragon. I found some pictures on the Internet, and he looks very much like them—except he's a lot smaller, doesn't breathe fire, and he's really nice."

"A dragon whose name is Roger," puzzled Aunt May. "You weren't getting enough sleep, were you? And you were probably eating pizza every day, so not getting enough vitamins."

"Oh, he's very real. Roger can talk, and he understands us—people, I mean."

"You are not just pulling my leg, are you? I was thinking you were just playing a trick on me, but you are serious. Well, let me meet this Roger then."

When he heard Aunt May say she wanted to see him, Roger flew around the corner of the wall where he had been hiding. He landed on the coffee table in front of Aunt May and Matthew.

"Oh my goodness!" cried Aunt May. "I've seen many odd, exotic, and foreign things, but I have never seen anything like you. You *are* real. And, you *do* look like a dragon!"

Roger had a hunch (sensitive dragon that he was, he had many hunches) that Aunt May would be able to understand him.

"I *am* a dragon," Roger told Aunt May. "My name is Roger."

Aunt May rubbed her forehead. "Matthew said that you could talk, and I just heard you speak. I could be suffering from jet lag, of course."

"I do not know what jet lag is," said Roger joyfully, "but you did hear me. You must be like Gail and believe in magic!"

"I *have* been told that I am young at heart and also that I am still like a child in many ways. I also believe in magic. There is magic all around us, in this world and in worlds beyond this, if only we open our hearts to it."

Roger stared at Aunt May with open awe. *Worlds beyond this one,* he mused. Roger turned these words over in his head. *I wonder if she is talking about the meadow,* he thought.

"I'm sorry, Roger," Aunt May said, breaking into Roger's thoughts. "Jet lag, which is an icky feeling I get after flying on a plane, must have affected my brain after all. Fancy me running on about magic like that. It is nice to meet you."

"You too," Roger replied shyly.

"Well." Aunt May stood up and rubbed her hands together. "All of this excitement has made me hungry. Is takeout okay with everyone? I'll order something other than pizza."

"So, Aunt May," said Matthew shyly after dinner, "may Roger stay?"

"Are you kidding? I wouldn't have him anywhere else."

Roger beamed at Aunt May. He liked his new friend.

Chapter 17

Kobe and Bear Go to the Magic Meadow

Roger's routine did not change after Aunt May's arrival. On nice days, Roger went outside in the morning and returned later in the afternoon. He always had lots of snacks and water left for him in a shady part of the yard. Roger usually visited with Sheila first, and then he would then fly to the ridge to visit with his friends there.

One warm afternoon, Roger was sitting with his friends in their favorite clearing when he suddenly thought of Kobe and Bear. *I haven't seen them for a long, long time*, he thought, scolding himself. *And I haven't told them about the meadow.*

"I am going to fly over to see Kobe and Bear," Roger announced. "I want to see how Kobe is doing."

"Would you like me and Soot to fly with you?" asked Jack.

Roger, feeling a little nervous about what he would find, thankfully agreed.

Roger and his two friends flew off and landed in the same tree as always. Roger saw his friends lying below. Roger immediately realized that something was off; Bear did not bark, and Kobe did not even raise his noble head. Roger quickly flew down.

Bear and Kobe were lying side by side. Roger knew about Kobe's legs, but he was baffled by Bear. Bear was not looking like his old, noisy self.

"Roger," Bear finally said, but it sounded like it took him great deal of effort to speak. "It is good to see you." Bear raised his head to peer up at the tree with blurry eyes. "And are those your friends up there?"

Kobe lifted his liquid brown eyes to Roger and said, "Yes, good to see you."

At that moment, Roger called his other friends down, and they all assembled around Kobe and Bear.

"Bear, Kobe!" Roger cried. "I am sorry that I have not been by to see you. Kobe, how are your legs? Bear, you don't look yourself!"

"I overheard my owners say that my legs will not recover," Kobe sadly replied. "I can barely scramble to my feet any longer."

"I became sick a couple of weeks ago," added Bear. "I will not get well either."

Roger, although saddened by this information, was glad that he had decided to visit this day.

"Do you know about the meadow?" asked Roger. He told the dogs about his conversations with Mel and Milly.

Kobe and Bear smiled at their relatively new friend and thanked him. "You've been a good friend." The dogs then exchanged a glance, and it seemed to Roger like a joint decision had been made.

They looked at Roger. "Good-bye," they chorused. They both then laid their heads back down and closed their eyes.

Roger looked back at Kobe and Bear. The dogs' forms seemed to shimmer for an instant.

"Kobe? Bear?" Roger asked haltingly.

"Roger," Jack said, "they can't hear you. They were ready for the meadow. They are there now. They will be like young puppies again. They can run, jump, and do all the things they used to before becoming ill. They're happy now."

"We should fly back," urged Soot. "We should tell the others."

With one last glance at Kobe and Bear, they all flew back to the clearing. The other three were all still there enjoying the sun.

"How did it go?" asked Jasper.

Roger told them how quickly Kobe and Bear found the meadow after they knew about it.

"They were very ready then for the meadow to find *them*," Jasper said. "And I believe every living being knows about the meadow in some manner. We forest animals are just more aware, as we are closer to nature and more sensitive about when the meadow is waiting. Sometimes I think it hovers just outside our thoughts for a long time before we realize it's there. I believe you did Kobe and Bear an enormous service by poking at those thoughts so they could see the meadow."

"Don't be sad, Roger," Jack added, eyeing the little dragon. "They're no longer in pain."

"Will I see them again?" Roger asked.

"Some of us believe we all go to the same meadow; it is endless, after all. Others believe the meadow shapes itself differently for each of us," Tip said. "We don't really know until we get there. I think it may be very likely that friends and family share the same meadow one day."

Roger thought about this for a moment. Even though he had not visited Kobe and Bear very often, he had grown fond of the gentle giants. He hoped he would see them again some day.

Roger realized he should fly home, as he had been gone for a while.

"Thank you so much for coming with me," Roger said to Jack and Soot. "I should be flying home now."

His friends said they would fly by later. Patch said he might scramble over later, as well. Tip was oddly silent.

Chapter 18

Tip

Roger flew home from the ridge in deep thought. He deeply wanted to tell Sugar and Ernie about Kobe and Bear. Once inside, he was puzzled when he could not find either cat. Roger decided to go in search of Matthew. *He will know where they are*, Roger thought.

He found Matthew in the kitchen surrounded by papers. He was muttering to himself.

"Oh hello, Roger," Matthew said absently, without looking up.

"What's going on?" Roger asked curiously.

"School is starting soon," Matthew explained. "I am getting my supplies organized."

Matthew finally pushed his chair back with a stretch and a sigh.

"There, I think I've got everything," he said.

Roger had been waiting patiently for Matthew to finish before he asked about Sugar and Ernie.

"Matthew, do you know where Sugar and Ernie are?"

"I had to lock Sugar in the downstairs family room for a time out. She was in one of her moods again. Ernie is probably hiding somewhere."

"May I go see her?"

"Well, I know that Sugar gets along with you, Ernie, and me—even when she is acting up—but it's supposed to be a time out. I think it is best if we leave her alone for a bit. If she is calmer later, I'll either let her out, or you can go visit her then."

Roger sighed and asked to go outside again. He decided to fly back to the ridge. *It will save my friends a trip here*, he thought. When he arrived, all of his friends were still in the clearing.

"Hi," he called. "What's going on?"

"It's Tip," sighed Jasper. "The birds and Patch were going to come see you later."

Roger glanced at the old hare; he was anxious about Tip's unusual silence.

"What is it, Tip?" Roger asked. He recalled that he had not seen Tip in Matthew's yard for a while. Tip usually could be seen nibbling on bushes.

Tip studied his front paws and said, "I'm very old. My hindquarters are paining me dreadfully; sometimes I cannot even hop. It's getting difficult to look for food. Winter is coming, and I know in my old rabbit bones that it will be very harsh for me."

"We can bring you food!" Roger cried. The others all nodded.

"No, my friends." Tip shook his grizzled head. "I am old. I think it's time for me to move on … I'll be in my warren." Tip hopped away with a limp.

Roger looked at the others in dismay.

"I think I can safely speak for all of us," Jasper said sadly, "in saying that we'll miss ole Tip. He has been a fixture on the ridge for a long time."

"I'll go after him," Roger said with determination. He quickly caught up with Tip, who was just nearing his comfortable warren. Roger noted that it was not far away from the clearing but well hidden.

"Roger," muttered Tip crossly. "It is always good to see you, but what are you doing here?"

"Well," stammered Roger. "I was just worried."

"I am going to have a long rest, but I'm not going into the meadow today. Would you all come to say farewell tomorrow? I'll wait. Now, I'm just going to lie down. Ah yes, there's some nice dried grass in here for me to munch on." Tip did precisely that; he lay on his side, with a mouthful of grass. Roger hurried back to the clearing.

Roger let the others know what Tip had said.

"Maybe we should go back now," Patch said in a worried voice.

"We'll honor his wishes and leave him be until tomorrow," Jasper decided. "I hope he waits for us."

"We'll go tomorrow. We'll go early," Jack said. "Tip said he'd wait, and he'll wait."

*****

After Roger left, Tip munched away on his grass and started thinking. "I am a fixture on the ridge," he said proudly to himself. "I'm glad I was asked to help look for the little eagle. Who knows the ridge better than I do?"

Tip finished his meal. "It's a pity my leg is acting up," he muttered aloud. "I guess it is time for me to hop along into the sunset."

The next morning, Tip felt himself able to hop again. Being his usual silly bunny self, Tip forgot that he had told his friends that he was ready for the meadow. "I'm hungry," Tip said to himself, and he hopped away in search of breakfast.

****

Roger flew home, hoping to see Sugar and Ernie sitting together on the sofa. Sadly, there was still no sign of either of them.

"Is Sugar still downstairs?" Roger asked Matthew.

"Yes. I did have her out, but then she started acting strangely once more. I had to lock her up again. Ernie is still hiding."

~ 95 ~

Roger's wee dragon's head was certainly full that night: Kobe and Bear, Tip, and now Sugar. He did not sleep very well at all. It was no problem, therefore, for him to be up early the next morning.

Roger led a solemn group to Tip's warren the next day. They had come to say farewell and see him off to the meadow. They arrived at Tip's home, but he was not there.

"Where did he go?" squeaked Roger. "He said he would wait for us."

Tip suddenly hopped back into his home.

"What are you all doing here?" Tip asked.

Roger spoke up immediately. He was delighted to see Tip looking so well. "Tip … we came to be with you,"

"Where were you?" demanded Jasper.

"We came to say good-bye to your furry little face," said Soot.

"I am so sorry," Tip began. "I forgot you were all going to come around this morning. I am ashamed that I made such a fuss. I woke up feeling a great deal better. *Wow*, I thought to myself, *this hare has some energy left, after all.*" Tip paused here. "And then I remembered; I remembered that while searching for Max, I caught my leg under a branch. I didn't think anything of it at the time; I guess I was just very involved with the search. The leg began to hurt, however, over the following days, and I thought— well, you know what I thought. I *am* old, and the cold *does* affect me more than it used to, but I have a few more hops in me. Besides, who would keep Patch in line if I wasn't around?"

"I'm just glad you're feeling better," said Roger.

"I think all of us are relieved," Jack added. "I, for one, was not ready to see my hoppy friend leave. I'm looking forward to spending another winter with you, and many other seasons."

"I'm flying home," Roger told his friends. "Will you be by later?"

All except Jasper, naturally, said they would be in Matthew's yard in the early afternoon.

"I'll not be as fast as I was," cautioned Tip, "but I will be there."

"I might even beat you," Patch teased and then scurried up a tree. "It's breakfast time! Roger, I hope your birdfeeder is full. I'm happy you are sticking around, my crusty old friend." This latter comment was directed to Tip, and Patch vanished within the leafy branches.

Chapter 19

Sugar

Roger flew home and landed outside the french doors. He was delighted to see that Sugar was sitting within, gazing out with a wistful expression on her pretty face. Seeing Roger, she pawed at the glass, and Aunt May appeared. She opened the doors for Roger, keeping one cautious hand on Sugar.

"Hi, Sugar!" Roger exclaimed happily.

"Hi, Roger!" Sugar replied, seeming equally happy.

Roger followed Sugar and found Ernie on the sofa. *Looks like things are back to normal,* Roger thought to himself. He was much relieved.

"I was looking for you two yesterday," Roger said.

"I had to be locked up downstairs," Sugar replied. "I am on some kind of kitty medicine to try to control my temper. At first I spit it out, but I realize it's good for me. I seem to be feeling better."

Roger was so relieved to see that Sugar was herself again that he forgot to tell her about the dogs and Tip. Roger and the cats settled on the sofa together.

****

School had started again, so Roger rarely saw Matthew. When he did see him, he was very grumpy. One thing Roger knew, Matthew still stayed up late playing video games. *No wonder he's grumpy,* Roger thought. The weather was changing, so Roger rarely saw his ridge friends either. He was content, however; he had Sugar, Ernie, and Aunt May to keep him company.

One afternoon, Roger, Sugar, and Ernie were nestled on the sofa. Outside, the sky had transformed from the beautiful robin's-egg blue, which was so characteristic of the skies in Alberta, to a sullen milky gray—an omen. The snow lords were busily gathering their fluffy clouds to toss upon the now barren plains. And snow it did—heavily.

Roger was astounded. Did this world never cease to offer wonders and surprises? What an astonishing day.

"What is that?" asked Roger. "It's all white and fluffy like popcorn!"

"That is snow," Ernie replied.

Roger thought of a recent visit to the ridge. He had noticed that Tip's coat was changing color. He had asked the old hare about it.

"Why, we rabbits change the color of our coats for winter, in order to blend in with the snow. That is so other animals cannot see us as well," Tip had replied.

"Oh, so *that's* snow," Roger said to Ernie. "The last time I was on the ridge, I noticed that Tip's coat seemed to be changing color; it was turning white. Tip told me that this change was in order to blend in with the snow. He said it also helped to hide rabbits from other critters. What is snow like?"

"It is sort of like rain—except colder. I hated it when I was a kitten," Ernie replied and looked at his white friend. "It never seemed to bother you, Sugar."

"I would like to be out there now." Sugar sighed. "It would be better for everyone. I have to tell you that I am not … right. I almost attacked Matthew yesterday. How could I even think of such a thing? What bothers me most is that I can't remember … all the time."

Roger and Ernie exchanged subtle glances, and Ernie snuggled a bit closer to his fat, furry white friend.

"I thought you were better," Roger said.

"As did I," Sugar replied. "But I overheard Matthew say that the medicine does not appear to be working very well."

Roger thought about his friends Kobe and Bear. He looked at Sugar, summoned his courage, and asked them if they knew about the meadow.

"The meadow?" queried Ernie. "What is that? I know that Sugar and I lived in what I guess were meadows when we were kittens. They were very pretty, except for the snow, rain, not having enough food, and hiding from other critters."

"Well," Roger began, his big eyes on Sugar, "I told you about the eagles, and Mel showing me the meadow? Mel, Milly, and all of my other ridge friends describe the meadow as very beautiful. I saw so myself. They said that everyone reaches the meadow as soon as they are ready to go there. I know you were not quite comfortable with my visits to Kobe and Bear, but Kobe and Bear are in their meadow now. I just thought it was time that I share that with you both. I really should have told you earlier."

****

Sugar stood, flexed, and trotted down to the lower family room. Sugar was thinking and thinking. Roger's story made little sense to her; she and Ernie had only been wild for six months of their lives before being rescued. The meadow seemed like a dream. She pounced upon her sofa, looked around, and decided to have a little nap.

A meadow sprung before her, full of wildflowers, butterflies, and two very large dogs. *Rats*, she thought, before bounding into the tall, fragrant grass and teasing Kobe and Bear.

Snow comes and snow goes in the city of Calgary. Sugar, like the snow, melted away that one afternoon—and was in her meadow, with Kobe and Bear.

****

Matthew came home on that fateful afternoon to find Ernie, Sugar, and Roger entwined on the sofa in the downstairs family room. Sugar appeared to be unusually quiet. Matthew leaned down and touched the pure white fur, stroked the sweet but at times scary face, and realized Sugar had moved on.

****

Roger glanced up at Matthew. He realized that he was trying to be brave.

"Sugar is happy," Roger said.

"I am happy for her then," Matthew replied. "I can't imagine that she was happy being locked up all the time."

*****

Epilogue

I would like to say that Sugar behaved herself in the meadow, but she delighted in tormenting her four-legged companions. Kobe and Bear actually enjoyed her company, although there was no way they were going to tell *her* that—she was pompous enough.

Winter rolled into Calgary slyly, a warm smile against the canvas of the sky, followed by a trembling frown, scattering snow like rice at a wedding reception.

Roger discovered that he very much liked hot chocolate and hot buttered popcorn. He remained at Matthew's house, and while missing his crazy, little white friend, he was certain that she was causing trouble in the meadow.

Printed in the United States
By Bookmasters